MW00813473

Simon Grave
and the Curious Incident of the Cat in the Daytime

Len Boswell

BLACK ROSE
writing™

© 2019 by Len Boswell

All rights reserved. No part of this book may be reproduced, stored in a retrieval system or transmitted in any form or by any means without the prior written permission of the publishers, except by a reviewer who may quote brief passages in a review to be printed in a newspaper, magazine or journal.

The final approval for this literary material is granted by the author.

First printing

This is a work of fiction. Names, characters, businesses, places, events and incidents are either the products of the author's imagination or used in a fictitious manner. Any resemblance to actual persons, living or dead, or actual events is purely coincidental.

ISBN: 978-1-68433-198-7
PUBLISHED BY BLACK ROSE WRITING
www.blackrosewriting.com

Printed in the United States of America
Suggested Retail Price (SRP) $18.95

Simon Grave and the Curious Incident of the Cat in the Daytime is printed in Palatino Linotype

To all I love without condition,
To all I love without omission.
Never doubt.

Simon Grave

and the Curious Incident of the Cat in the Daytime

"If man could be crossed with the cat it would improve the man, but it would deteriorate the cat."
—Mark Twain

"Each life makes its own imitation of immortality."
—Stephen King

"The problem with cats is that they get the same exact look whether they see a moth or an ax-murderer."
—Paula Poundstone

"I'll go get the horse and buggy," you'll say. And I'll say, "But I thought we were taking the hovercraft?"
—David Levithan

Prologue

For many years, nay centuries, Crab Cove, a town on the Eastern Shore of Maryland, has moved unhampered by progress. Even now, in the latter part of the twenty-first century, the crab boats still use traps and nets and trotlines to bring home the blue crabs that define the town in every way. It is said of the town that Crab Cove is a place where change comes to die and anachronisms come to spawn.

So as the rest of the world flies in cars and waits eagerly for news from the burgeoning Mars Colony, the residents of Crab Cove and the Greater Crabopolis focus on the crab harvest and the distribution of he-crabs and she-crabs—*jimmies* and *sooks*—and gripe about the increasing intrusion of tourists, technology, and people fleeing to higher ground from the incursion of the seas, despite the fact that the town's livelihood depends on all of them.

Change is a bitch to most Crab Cove residents, but she is a goddess to others. Two camps have emerged, those wishing to stay in the distant past, hoping to keep time in a bottle or at least a crab trap, and those seeking to push the town into at least the near past, where people can enjoy hover cars, designer organs—organoids—and other already-displaced technology.

The no-change faction has held sway for years, but the bitch-goddess of change isn't satisfied, introducing a corporation, Ramrod Robotics, that has changed Crab Cove forever. The changes were slight at first, the company introducing robotic lawnmowers and vacuum cleaners to the town, which it grudgingly accepted, at least on a small scale.

But everything changed two years ago. Two young women had been murdered at the Hawthorne mansion, home to Darius Hawthorne, the founder and CEO of Ramrod Robotics, now serving a life term for the murders, along with his wife, Philomena, who is the sister of the still-at-large serial killer Chester Clink. But as horrific as the murders were, the principal thing that had attracted the attention of the town was the involvement of robots in the killings.

Suddenly, almost everyone in town seemed to be dead set on owning a robot, or simdroid as they are called, androids that simulate the voice and appearance of famous people—actors, singers, politicians, you name it—or of anyone, including deceased loved ones. They can be programmed to do anything. They can be crabbers, they can be doctors, they can be household servants, they can be auto mechanics, they can be sexbots, they can be *anything.*

The bitch-goddess has brought progress, yes, but she has also brought strife. More and more, business owners are replacing their human workers with simdroids, who are faster and more efficient, and don't take smoke breaks or bitch about the coffee in the break room.

And with this strife comes tension, and with this tension comes crime, and with this crime comes almost-handsome Detective Simon Grave and his partner, Sergeant Barry Blunt, a man so nondescript he is almost invisible, a man neither here nor there, but probably standing next to you right now.

Crab Cove, in short, is neither a utopia nor a dystopia, but something other. Sociologists, who can be found on the streets of Crab Cove in great number on any given day, are of different minds on just what kind of *topia* Crab Cove is. *Bitopia, extratopia, hypertopia, intratopia, contratopia, cornucopiatopia, midtopia, kaleidotopia, collidotopia,* and *polytopia* are terms that fill the pages of thesis after thesis. But perhaps the closest match to what is going on is an *asynchronotopia,* a place where anything and everything seems out of place and out of time, where competing worlds coexist in a perpetual tug-of-war, each striving to win out against the other.

Where a utopia brings peace and abundance, and a dystopia brings dysfunction and want, an *asynchronotopia* brings an anachronistic mélange of competing customs, beliefs, and inventions, and in a town like Crab Cove, where the past is as present as the future, a sense that something is not quite right, like an olive in your coffee.

Of course, Detective Simon Grave couldn't care less about what kind of *topia* Crab Cove is. If you press him, he might say that Crab Cove is a *bizarrotopia*, but if you ask him why, he certainly won't be able to tell you. Deep thought is simply not part of his skill set. To him, whatever happens in Crab Cove is just Crab Cove being Crab Cove. And he's fine with that.

1

Her long-sleeved black dress and preternaturally tiny waist gave her the appearance of a segmented insect as she scurried through the buzzing crowd from food station to food station, gnawing at cheeses and nibbling at hors d'oeuvres, her head on a swivel, looking for the next delectable morsel or more, perhaps a whole ham or prime rib of beef she could grasp in her mandibles and drag back to the nest. Detective Simon Grave looked down at his empty wine glass, his third, then set it aside on a nearby tray. Enough was enough.

The first day of the 17th Annual Crab Cove Conference on Crime, or C4 as it was known in the law enforcement community, had gone about as expected, with one boring lecture leading inexorably to an even more boring workshop, interrupted only by brief bathroom breaks where attendees had to choose between relieving their bladders or filling up on coffee and donuts supplied by Crab Cove's nearly famous Skunk 'n Donuts.

Fortunately for Grave—and perhaps explaining his indulgence in more than a single glass of chardonnay at the cocktail reception—his own part in the conference, a lecture on his most recent case, The Hawthorne Mansion Murders, had gone well and was thankfully over. The audience of fellow professionals had seemed rapt by his description of the murders, the role played by simdroids, and the ultimate conclusion to the case. Only one person had asked him a question, and he had handled it easily.

Or so he thought.

He could see the questioner, a detective from Baltimore, working his way toward him, which made him instinctively snatch another glass of wine from the tray of a waiter working his way through the crowd. He took a sip, braced himself, and offered his best attempt at an indulgent, welcoming smile.

The man launched right in. "I've been giving your answer some thought, and I can't help wondering about it."

"Oh," said Grave, "in what way?" He glanced over the man's shoulder, where he could see that his boss, Captain Henry Morgan, had spotted him and was heading his way with some purpose, which was never a good thing.

"That a detective's job is more about *revealing* logic than using logic," the man said. "I find that illogical."

Grave took a long sip of wine, trying to polish it off before Morgan reached him. "Well, nothing is absolute, of course, even with logic."

"So you say, but—"

Captain Morgan interrupted, stepping between them and pulling Grave aside.

"Come," he said to Grave, "we have a body."

Grave didn't need to be asked twice, and was happy to be rescued, giving the Baltimore detective a shrug and a wave, and moving quickly through the crowd with Captain Morgan, the effect of the wine creating a blur of people and a whir of sound as he tried to keep pace.

Then he had a pertinent thought. "I didn't bring my car."

Captain Morgan's enormous face suddenly appeared in front of his. "No need. The body is just outside, on the beach. Sergeant Blunt is securing the area, and I've made a call for the medical examiner."

"Polk or Withers?" His voice sounded strange. Had he slurred *Withers?*

"Polk, of course. Or have you forgotten that Withers retired."

"Oh, right. That medical thingy."

Morgan nodded and took his best shot at a reverential, solemn tone, which was a stretch for a man who personified gruff. "Yes, inoperable tumor. Damned shame."

He gave Grave an appraising look. "You all right?"

Grave tried his best to put on a non-tipsy look. "Yes, I'm fine."

"You seem a bit wobbly."

"The wine, yes, I'll be fine. Just point me in the right direction."

They made their way through the lobby and out through the revolving doors, Morgan grabbing him by the arm and turning him sharply left. Grave could see the lights around the murder scene and a grayish cloud hovering over a body. That would be Sergeant Blunt, a man so nondescript he was invisible to all but the practiced eye, looking more like a mist or a cloud than a man.

Four simdrones were hovering over the site, providing additional light, and Grave could see a few more flying along the beach, searching the shoreline. The use of robots had exploded after the Hawthorne case, and the local manufacturer, Ramrod Robotics, had been more than eager to provide simdroids—robots that closely resembled famous people—to the masses. The people of Crab Cove could simply not get enough of them, and the police force was no exception. Simdroid patrolmen had been added to the force, mostly to handle parking violations; and then there were the simdrones, highly advanced drones no bigger than a Frisbee that provided enhanced search and apprehension capabilities. Grave, a self-confessed Luddite, was having a hard time keeping up with the new technology.

His cellphone, a new and maddeningly non-intuitive iPhone 37 Police, began to ring and vibrate in his pocket. He pulled it out and fumbled with it, finally coaxing it to life. His father was calling, again.

"My father," he said, turning it off and sliding it back into his pocket.

Morgan, who was no fan of Grave's father, the former Detective Jacob Grave, now retired, grunted his disapproval and picked up the pace.

Grave was happy to be outside in the evening air, which though still warm, was infinitely cooler than the air in the people-packed conference center ballroom. He could feel the effects of the wine lessen as he raced to catch up with Morgan, who had suddenly stopped twenty yards ahead. The scene, save for Sergeant Blunt, came into sharp focus: a body spread-eagled on a blanket in the sand, a simdroid standing beside it, motionless. *Robots?* he thought. *Again?*

2

She stood apart, lurking in the darkness along the shore, and watched the two men approach and walk into the bright light of the crime scene. She recognized the tall, square-jawed Detective Grave immediately, the curious Dudley Do-Right of a man who had made the presentation earlier in the day. She had spent the entire lecture trying to figure out why she was attracted to him. He certainly wasn't handsome, at least not in the traditional sense, but there was something about him—his pale blue eyes, his thick black hair, his speed bump of a nose, and the way his eyes crinkled when he smiled—that made her feel a deep heat.

The other man seemed to be Grave's antithesis. He was short and stocky, with a block-like head and a flattened blob of a nose that suggested he had run into a wall at great speed. Even so, she could tell by the way the men were interacting that this other man was Grave's superior.

Grave was the first to spot her, and motioned her forward. She picked up her shoes where she had left them in the sand and walked into the light, trying her best not to look at the man lying there.

Grave was startled to see the segmented insect from the cocktail party, who now stood before him, an insect turned woman, and a beautiful woman at that, albeit a very thin one. She was one of those bony, hollow-cheeked young women you would see on fashion runways, the kind you wished would eat a cookie. Her eyes, which appeared to be larger than life, given the thinness of her face, were lavender and set wide above a long, thin nose that may have been the result of surgery. She had pulled her black hair into a tight bun, which had certainly done nothing to dispel her insect look. All she needed was antennae. "Um, I understand you were the one who found the body?"

She extended her hand. "Yes, Pippa Wobbly. I was trying to walk off some of those hors d'oeuvres from the party."

She wiped the corner of her mouth, hoping there were no traces of the food she had thrown up into the lapping waves along the beach. "I so enjoyed your lecture."

Grave took her hand, which was thin and cold. He had the feeling he could crush it with little effort. "Thank you. Now, tell us what you saw. How you happened upon the body."

She smiled up at him. "As I said, I had eaten far too much, so I thought a walk on the beach would be just the thing. And then, there he was. I practically tripped over him."

"Did you see or hear anyone leaving the scene? Anything?"

"No, nothing. Anyway, I called 911, and here we are."

"And why are you here, Ms. Wobbly?" said Captain Morgan. "Attending the conference?"

"Well, yes, sort of. I'm the new reporter at the *The Claw & Mallet*."

Morgan couldn't help rolling his eyes. The local paper had been the bane of his existence, so he certainly didn't want her snooping around the crime scene. "Well, then, we may want to talk with you further, but you can go now. Leave your contact information with Sergeant Blunt, and we'll be in touch."

Wobbly looked around. "Who?"

"Me," said a disembodied voice in front of her.

She tried her best to make out the man, but he seemed to be no more formed than a vapor.

"Don't worry, ma'am," said Blunt. "I get that all the time."

She squinted in the direction of the voice, vague outlines of a large man coming into fuzzy focus. "Oh, there you are."

She turned back to Grave and Morgan. "I'd like to stay, if you don't mind. As a reporter."

Captain Morgan shook his head. "No, I'm afraid that will not be possible. Integrity of the crime scene, you see."

"I see. Well, then, will you at least grant me an exclusive, given that I discovered the body?"

Morgan smirked at her. "You already know more than any other reporter." He glanced around, knowing that TV trucks would be arriving any minute. "And you have a head start. Write what you know, and I'm sure you'll be well ahead of the game."

Wobbly frowned. "As you wish." She looked back and forth between Morgan and Grave, and gave them a little smile. "Well, then, I'll say goodnight."

She turned and walked out of the light, trailed by the cloud that was Sergeant Blunt.

Morgan watched her go, then turned to Grave. "Just what we need. A reporter as witness."

"And here come the rest," said Grave, pointing back toward the conference center, where several TV trucks were pulling into the parking lot, their antennae and satellite disks moving into position.

"Oh, Christ," said Morgan.

3

Jeremy Polk, the medical examiner, went about his work in silence, examining the body with great care and grunting from time to time as if he had noticed something unexpected, or at least significant enough for a grunt.

He was a small man, but held himself in a way that suggested a much taller small man. The effect was so startling, your first reaction was to look down at his feet to see if he was on tiptoe, which he never was. Captain Morgan called it a Napoleonic stance. Grave called it hall-of-mirrors weird.

Finally, Grave could not stand another grunt. "Okay, Polk, what have you got?"

Polk peered up at him, his beady, close-set eyes narrowing even further. "A moment," he said, then turned back to the body, sniffing at it like a hound with his little pug nose, which was gray and shiny, like a fish washed up on the beach.

"What is it?" said Grave.

Polk stood and stretched himself up to his full height, which still required that he strain his neck in order to look up into the face of Detective Grave. "Crabs."

"Crabs?" said Grave.

"Yes, he smells of crabs."

"Polk, the entire population of Crab Cove smells like crabs."

"No, you misunderstand me. He absolutely *reeks* of crabs, from his shoes to his hair. Even has a little crabmeat under his fingernails. He's a crab worker of some kind. A picker, I would think."

Captain Morgan leaped to the obvious, which was a special talent of his. "So he worked at Crab Cove Pick 'n Pack, right?"

Polk turned to Morgan and smiled. "Very perceptive, Cap'n."

Morgan, a natural sponge for praise, beamed back.

"So what else?" said Grave.

"Well, it's all a bit odd, or maybe it's nothing at all. No signs of trauma whatsoever, which suggests this old man just gave up the ghost here on the beach. A heart attack or some such." He paused. "Then again."

"Yes?" said Grave. He knew Polk was teasing him.

"Then again, his wallet is missing and there are clear drag marks that run from the parking lot to this spot."

Grave looked quickly around. He hadn't even noticed the marks, but there they were, along with deep, wide footprints that could only be made by a simdroid, most likely the one slumped over near the body, motionless.

"So the simdroid dragged the body here? Why would it do that?"

Polk shook his head. "No, look at her. She's small, petite even for a droid. Reminds me of an old actress. I'm not sure which one. Anyway, to the point, the droid prints are too far away from the drag marks, and—"

"What about these?" Grave pointed at a set of smaller prints that seemed to weave back and forth across the droid prints.

Polk gave out a little puff of exasperation. "Really? They're obviously from a small animal. A cat or small dog, I would suspect."

"Do you think?"

"No," said Polk with a firm shake of his head. "*Not* related. *Not* important. May I continue?"

Grave nodded and took a step back, which Polk seemed to appreciate.

"So," Polk continued, "the droid was walking along, following whoever was dragging the body, a person who had the good sense to wipe away his own footprints, coming and going." He looked at the droid again. "Of course, maybe the droid came later."

Grave thought to ask when the small animal might have come along, but thought better of it, giving Captain Morgan a chance to weigh in.

"What *about* the droid, then?"

"It's curious," said Polk, walking over to it. "See here, its dipstick thingy is missing."

Grave knew exactly what that was: a *simcortex*, a thin device that activated a droid when it was inserted into its back and that deactivated the droid when it was removed. Everything that made a simdroid what it was—programming, memory, capabilities, and personality—was stored on that device.

Grave nodded. "So the killer removed it, right?"

Morgan joined the nodding. "And it's *gone?* "

"Yes and yes," said Polk. "Buried, thrown into the bay, or carried away."

Morgan threw up his hands. "Crap!"

"I'll put the simdrones to work on that," said Grave, reaching for his phone. "If it's here, they'll find it."

Several swipes, pushes, and miscues later, the phone came to life with a series of beeps that summoned one of the simdrones that had been scanning the beach.

A simdrone broke from its pattern and whirred its way to them, coming to a hovering stop in front of Grave's face. "Sir," it said.

The voice was unmistakable: Morgan Freeman, a famous actor, now long dead, but with a voice that lived on. One of the signature features of all simdroids and simdrones manufactured by Ramrod Robotics was their distinctive voice programming. Buyers could select from more than a thousand voices of actors, actresses, singers, world leaders, or other personalities. The Crab Cove Police Force had selected Morgan Freeman's voice for all their simdroids and simdrones. And all the police simdroids actually looked like Morgan Freeman, who personified just the quality of authority they were looking for.

"What is your name?" asked Grave. He didn't need to ask—all the simdrones had the same name. It just made life easier, and they didn't seem to mind.

The simdrone whirred and clicked. "Larry."

"All right, Larry, I have an assignment for you and the other simdrones."

"Anything, sir. I fly to serve."

"Good. I assume you are familiar with simcortexes."

"Yes."

Grave pointed at the motionless simdroid. "This simdroid here is missing its simcortex. I want you and the other simdrones to scan this beach and as far out into the bay as you deem appropriate to find it."

Larry dipped his front propellers down to simulate a nod, then wobbled a bit to indicate he was in deep thought. "Yes, sir, given the weight of a simcortex for this model and the maximum throwing distance by a top athlete, that would be exactly 131.758 feet. We'll adjust that upward to 175.637 feet, given the known currents here."

"That works for me," said Grave.

Larry whirred loudly and lifted away to begin the scan.

Grave turned back to Polk. "Has anyone taken overhead photos of the crime scene?"

"No, not yet," said Polk.

Grave pulled out his phone again. "Okay, I'm on it."

One of the features of his phone was that it could fly and hover, at least across short distances. He pressed a few buttons, and the phone lifted from his hands, hovered over the scene, clicked off ten clean shots of the scene, and returned to his hand.

Actually, that is what was *supposed* to happen. What actually happened was nothing. The phone just sat there in his hand. He puffed his cheeks and set about pressing a different combination of buttons, which also did nothing. Frustrated, he pressed in yet another combination and tossed the phone into the air, hoping it would perform. Instead, it arced above the scene and fell edge down in the sand, looking like a tortilla chip stuck in guacamole.

Captain Morgan looked at the phone in the sand and shook his head. "You really should consider some remedial training on that thing, Grave."

Grave nodded meekly as Morgan's own phone lifted into the air and quickly completed the task.

Grave turned back to Polk. "Now, then, anything *else* we should know?"

Polk sighed. "I'll know more when I get him back to the morgue. Run some tests. I think toxicology will win the day."

Morgan squinted at him. "So, poison?"

Polk tapped the simdroid on the shoulder. "More likely an injection, an overdose of prescribed medicine."

Captain Morgan looked puzzled. "Why would you say that?"

"The simdroid, sir. If I am not mistaken, it is a Simdroid 3500 HP."

Morgan scowled, frustrated. "And that means?"

"The HP stands for *hospice partner*. It's a simdroid that assists people who are dying, providing pleasant conversation and administering pain killers as needed."

Morgan seemed satisfied. "Oh, okay."

But Grave wasn't. "Wait, so you think it's The Hawthorne Mansion Murders all over again? Simdroids who can kill?"

Polk shrugged. "It's possible, I guess, but the new programming protocols put in place after those murders would suggest that these new simdroids could do no harm. More likely that someone may have tampered with the simcortex somehow."

"And that would take expertise," said Grave.

"Yes, of course," said Polk. He looked back at the body and the simdroid. "Look, if we're done here, I'd like to get the body back to the morgue."

"Fine," said Captain Morgan. "Do you need the simdroid? We could take it back to the station, wait to see if the simwhatsit thingy can be found."

"No," said Polk. "We'll want to check it for prints and DNA."

Morgan nodded. "Oh, right. Well, then, take them both, and let us know when you have something. If we find anything, we'll let you know and send it along."

Polk turned without comment and motioned his assistants to

move the body and the simdroid into the waiting van.

Captain Morgan heaved a big sigh. "Well, I guess we're done here, at least for now. Do you need a ride home?"

Grave was about to say yes, but then he saw, or thought he saw, Sergeant Blunt returning to the beach.

"Um, no sir. I'll get a ride with Blunt, bring him up to speed on what we know."

"Very well, I'll be on my way."

Grave watched him trudge back toward the conference center, which now seemed surrounded by TV trucks. In the bright lights near one of the vans he spotted the woman he least wanted to see: Claire Fairly, the TV reporter who had hounded him during the Hawthorne mansion case. Her look was unmistakable, from her close-cropped blond hair to her penchant for red, tightfitting skirts that emphasized her long, shapely legs, made longer by four-inch heels. At forty-seven, she was still beautiful, but the effects of aging were catching up to her more and more each year. One sign of that was the red scarf around her neck, no doubt to cover up wrinkles.

"Shit," he said, turning away and looking down the beach.

Larry the Simdrone was hovering over a spot twenty yards out into the bay, his claw probe descending into the water. It reminded Grave of one of those old-fashioned claw machines at the Crab Cove Arcade and Gaming Museum. He just hoped Larry's claw was more powerful than the weak ones in those machines, which had taken many a quarter from the slow-to-learn Detective Grave, who had failed miserably in his attempt to come away with an action figure of Pootaka Slyth, the arch villain in Star Wars XXVI.

Grave's flight-challenged phone began to ring again. He picked it out of the sand, brushed the sand away, and turned it off. *Not now*, he thought, *not now.*

4

Larry the Simdrone had come through for them, the simcortex now bagged and tagged and sitting on the lap of Detective Grave, who was trying his best not to hyperventilate as the cloud beside him drove the car through the streets of Crab Cove, a town that had changed in so many ways in the past two years.

The explosion in the use of robotics had changed a quaint little crabbing and vacation town into a rapidly growing crabopolis, where humans and simdroids, seemingly in equal number, worked and played. And since simdroids could resemble anyone in history, the town seemed to occupy a space in time involving multiple centuries. On any five-minute walk down Main Street, you could see Thomas Jefferson, Abe Lincoln, Richard Nixon, and a host of actors and singers, from Cary Grant to Justin Timberlake—even new stars like Quake, who was topping the neodisco charts with his new song, "Simmed Out."

Not that simdroids were uniformly embraced. The pickers at Crab Cove Pick 'n Pack, for example, now had to compete with simdroid pickers, who were faster and more efficient than their human counterparts. The simdroids, in short, had insinuated themselves into every aspect of Crab Cove life, and some residents feared they were taking over.

Grave couldn't help but wonder out loud whether the Hawthorne murders and the attendant publicity around them had had something to do with this competition.

"It's possible, sir," said Sergeant Blunt.

Grave returned to the case. "We'll have to check out the Pick 'n Pack, at least once we figure out who the victim is."

"So, should we go to the morgue now?"

"No, we can wait until morning. I'm sure Captain Morgan will want to tag along."

"Very good, then, I'll just drop you at home."

They fell silent for some minutes, but finally the passage of time reached that awkward moment where silence seemed just the wrong thing, like a clown at a gravesite.

Grave felt compelled to say something, anything, so he decided to ask about Blunt's wife, June, who was pregnant with their first child and approaching the delivery zone. June was the spokesperson for Ramrod Robotics and had been instrumental in solving the Hawthorne murders. Like Blunt, she was so nondescript she was barely visible. The odd thing was that each of them could see the other clearly. They were simply meant for each other.

"So," said Grave, "how is June?"

"Well, thanks, but honestly, she looks like she's going to deliver a watermelon."

Grave laughed. "Or maybe several cantaloupes."

"No, no, just a single watermelon, at least according to the ultrasound."

"She's getting close, right?"

"Yes, any day now." His voice quavered.

"You seem nervous."

Blunt chuckled. "Yeah, I'm a bit on edge. First time jitters."

Grave reached over and patted the cloud, hoping he was patting Blunt's shoulder. "Don't worry. I'm sure it will be just fine. Look, turn left here."

Blunt braked and made a sharp left onto Grave's street.

"Sorry, almost missed it," said Blunt.

"No problem. Here we go, third house on the right."

Blunt slowed the car and came to a stop in front of Grave's house, an old bungalow that had been flipped into smart-house modernity, a house where every switch and socket, every lamp and appliance seemed to be sentient. At times, Grave thought the house was smarter than he was and out to get him, particularly his toaster, which created blackened toast regardless of setting.

"Here you go, sir." Blunt glanced over at Grave's car, an old red Austin Healy Sprite parked in the driveway. "How's the car behaving?"

"Actually, never better. Charlize has it running like a top."

"I must confess, sir, I never figured you for a simdroid owner."

Grave had thought the same himself, until that day when June had shown him the new line of simdroids, and he had been smitten by a model that simulated the young Charlize Theron, an actress who now spent her days in a retirement home, making do with occasional income from hearing-aid-implant commercials.

She was a Simdroid 4000 and had been programmed to serve a variety of functions, from cleaning, to cooking, to driving, to any number of household duties. Given Grave's occupation, she had also been programmed for detection, logical thought, psychological profiling, and donut humor. Most important, though, she was an auto mechanic, with special skills in the repair and maintenance of Austin Healy Sprites.

"I know, Blunt, but she is just amazing."

"Does she, um, you know?"

Grave didn't know where Blunt was going. "What?"

"Um, you know, perform any *wifely* duties."

Grave gulped. It had been months since he had enjoyed the pleasures of the bed, thanks to his breakup with Lola LaFarge, the French governess at Hawthorne Mansion. One day everything had been fine, and the next, she was on a plane back to Paris without even leaving a note. He had done something wrong, perhaps terribly wrong, but he didn't know what, and she refused to answer his calls.

He unclicked his seat belt. "No, as tempting as it was, I opted out of that feature."

Blunt was sorry he asked. "Of course, sir, of course."

Grave stepped out of the car. "All right, Blunt, I'll see you in the morning."

"Do you need a ride, sir?"

"No, Charlize will drive me in."

"See you at the station, then."

"Right." Grave closed the car door and watched as Blunt pulled away and turned the corner. He headed up the sidewalk, the house flickering to life as it always did when he got within twenty feet of the front door, which now opened, Charlize silhouetted in the doorway, a glass of his favorite wine, Duct Tape Chardonnay ("the wine that can fix anything") in her hand, ready to hand it to him. Life was good.

His phone began to ring again. He didn't have to guess who it was. *Dad, dad, dad.*

The glass of wine was just what he needed to put a cap on the evening, and seeing Charlize was always a good thing, except perhaps for her penchant for new clothes, which was playing havoc with his bank account.

Once again, she had greeted him at the door in a brand new outfit, including tight-fitting ultrayoga pants and a matching silver top that made him question his decision to forgo consort programming. Her love of clothes was completely counter to his own feeling about clothes, which was clearly evident to anyone looking in his closet, home for a dozen gray suits. Lola had tried her best to add variety to his wardrobe, buying him a half-dozen Hawaiian shirts, but they mostly languished at the back of the closet.

She caught the lustful look. "You know, I can be upgraded to provide whatever you desire."

Grave frowned. "Is it that obvious?"

"Yes, you flush a little, and that little gasp of a sigh is a dead giveaway. How long has it been now?"

"I don't know, months, I guess."

"You're pushing the statistical envelope, Simon. Too much longer and it will affect your work. Are you sure I can't help, even for a night? I'm fully functional down there, you know. All I lack is love-making techniques and the ability to simulate passion and orgasm."

"I know that, but no."

Charlize forced a well-programmed, nuanced smile and guided him to the couch. "Here, sit down a minute."

He sat down, but rather than sitting next to him, she positioned herself on the floor, cross-legged in front of him. "Perhaps I *am* too beautiful for you. You know you can return me at any time, change me out for something different."

Grave nodded, then shook his head and looked away from her. "No, I will not do that."

Charlize sighed, frustrated. "Did you at least try to chat someone up at the conference?"

"No."

"And you weren't attracted to a single woman there?"

Grave thought about the insect-woman, Pippa Wobbly. "Well, maybe, but the situation wasn't quite right."

"Situation?"

Now it was Grave's turn to sigh. "Another murder."

Charlize brightened. There was nothing she looked forward to more than a new case to test her analytical skills. "Will you need my help?"

"Of course, but we will have to be circumspect, as usual. Captain Morgan is not a fan of simdroid detectives, as you well know."

Grave wondered whether he shared Morgan's view. His job would be on the line one day, he was sure of it. Still, Charlize had a way of approaching cases that was so thorough and analytical that it made him wonder about his own abilities, even given his success rate.

"Is it Chester Clink again?"

The whole subject of Chester Clink was a sore point. His father, Jacob Grave, had failed to catch the killer, who was now responsible for the deaths of 77 young women, including two in the past month. Grave's own efforts had led nowhere as well. The man was incredibly elusive. And to make matters worse, Captain Morgan had pulled him from the investigation, giving the lead to a newly hired detective, Amanda Snoot, who seemed to delight in outlining his false steps in each of the Clink murder investigations.

"No," he said. "A body on the beach this evening, right at the conference center. And a simdroid seems to have been involved." He held up the evidence bag containing the simcortex.

She reached out for it. "Let me see that."

He handed it to her.

She turned it this way and that. "Hmm, a hospice partner, 3500 series."

"Yes, the simcortex had been removed and thrown into the bay."

She handed the bag back to Grave. "I see. Look, I've prepared a late dinner for you, on the chance that you'd be hungry, which you always are. Then we can discuss this in more detail. I'll access what I know about the 3500s, and we can proceed from there."

Grave nodded. "Fine, anything else going on here today?"

Charlize beamed. "I put in new spark plugs, checked the engine timing, and lubed the SU carbs. I think you'll see the difference in the morning."

"You didn't fix the radio, did you?"

When Grave had received the car from his father, the radio had been stuck on one channel at full volume. When he started the car, the radio came on automatically, and there was no way to shut it off without turning off the car. He had hated it at first, but then it had begun to grow on him.

Charlize frowned. "No, although I wish you'd reconsider. There's more to life than the Reverend Bendigo Bottoms and his gospel music."

Grave wasn't so sure. He had actually met the reverend during The Hawthorne Mansion Murders case, and they had had a long conversation at Skunk 'n Donuts about life, which the reverend thought was just like a tuna fish sandwich. Grave had agreed with him insofar as the bread and tuna were concerned, but he had had his doubts—no, strong reservations—about the mayonnaise as a life construct. Despite their disagreements about religion and the meaning of life, they had struck up a friendship—even shared a chocolate donut, which to Grave was a much worthier life totem.

"But I like him," said Grave, "*and* the loud singing. It helps me think."

Charlize rolled her eyes. "Whatever. It's a ten-minute fix. Just let me know."

Grave shook his head and quickly changed the subject. "So, anything *else* happening?"

Charlize shrugged. "Phone calls. Captain Morgan says to meet him at the morgue first thing. Oh, and your father keeps calling and calling."

Grave looked alarmed. "You didn't answer, did you?"

Charlize looked hurt. "No, of course not. I follow your instructions with complete faithfulness, you know that."

As if on cue, Grave's phone began to ring and vibrate.

"Oh, Christ!"

"You should answer it. He's never going to stop."

Grave sighed. She was right. He pulled the phone out of his pocket and fumbled it to life. "Hello, Dad."

There was a brief pause, as if his father was startled that he had actually gotten through. "Simon, is that you?"

"Who else would it be, Dad?"

"Never mind. Now listen."

"This isn't about Chester Clink is it? You know I've been pulled off the case."

"No, I know that."

"Then what?"

There was another pause. He could hear his father's breathing become more labored. "Dad, are you okay?"

"Simon, we have to *talk.*"

"Okay, shoot."

Another pause. "No, not on the phone. It's important, and *personal*. Could you stop by tomorrow morning?"

His father's voice sounded strange, which alarmed him. "Dad, what is it?"

Another unusual pause. "No, come tomorrow." He hung up.

Charlize could see the concern on Simon's face. "What, what is it?"

"I don't know. He sounded worried, which is not like him."

She offered her hand. "Come on, let's get some food into you, and we can talk—about *everything*."

Her hand was so lifelike, so warm, that he began to have second and third thoughts about his decision not to upgrade.

Say what you will about Charlize's clothes-bingeing habits, she always dressed for the occasion. She was a chauffeur this morning, so she dressed like one, right down to the tailored black suit and matching gloves and hat. Her long blond hair streamed behind her like an aviator's scarf as they cruised down the highway on their way to the morgue.

Reverend Bendigo Bottoms had just finished his commandment for the day, a well-reasoned argument on the evils of chipotle, and the gospel singers were shrieking at full volume on the merits and love of their Lord.

Charlize turned her head and shouted into Grave's ear. "Don't forget to ask the questions."

Grave nodded and yelled back. "I won't."

They drove on in silence, working their way through the morning traffic, cars yielding to them and dropping back to get away from the sound. Ten minutes later they were in the morgue parking lot. Charlize pulled into a space next to two patrol cars and turned off the engine.

"Did you notice how smooth it was, the acceleration?" she said.

"Yes, quite an improvement."

"It's the timing. It was off by a degree of top-dead-center."

Grave had no idea what she was talking about, and she knew it. "All right," she said. "I'll wait here. Go do your thing."

"You could come in, you know, so long as you're quiet."

"No, we can talk about what you find later. I don't want to annoy Captain Morgan."

Grave knew she would. She had no filter when it came to logical argument, and thought Morgan was "logic challenged." She considered him a conclusion jumper, someone who took the first piece of evidence and rolled it toward an illogical, and wrong, conclusion. And she was right. That's exactly what Morgan did, time and time again.

He unbuckled himself and opened the door. "Okay, this shouldn't take too long."

"No worries. I'll run my routine maintenance checks, clear out superfluous data, and get ready for some deep analysis."

Grave grunted his approval, got out of the car, and walked into the morgue, which seemed to have its own weather system, cold air buffeting him as he opened the door to the examination room. And that smell, that cloyingly sweet smell of antiseptic and death. Morgan and Blunt hovered near the table, watching Polk point and poke at the body.

Captain Morgan looked up briefly. "There you are. We're already into it."

"Anything yet?" said Grave.

"Not much from the body yet," said Polk, "but we found a couple of brochures in his pocket that may be of interest."

"Brochures?"

"For cemeteries," said Blunt.

Grave shrugged. "Not unusual for a man in hospice, though."

"No," said Polk, "but he's scribbled appointment times on the brochures. He met with both of them yesterday, it seems, just hours before we found him on the beach."

"Okay, we'll have to check them out. Did you find anything else?"

Polk cleared his throat. "Yes and no."

Grave sighed heavily. "It's always yes and no with you."

Polk chuckled. "It's as much an art as a science, Grave. Sometimes facts and observations *conflict.*"

"No lectures, please. What have you found—*yes and no?*"

"*Yes*, it was definitely an overdose, but *no*, we don't know exactly what yet."

Grave lifted the bagged simcortex in front of Polk's face. "Perhaps this will help." He looked around the room, looking for the hospice-partner simdroid, which he could see was slumped in the far corner.

"Blunt, hook her up and let's have a chat. Who is she supposed to be, anyway? I don't recognize her."

Captain Morgan piped up. "Oh, that's Betty White, an actress who died, what, forty years ago? Very popular, everyone loved her. Seems like a perfect choice for a hospice partner."

Grave squinted at her, then laughed. "Oh, right, I see it now. Okay, let's wake her up and see what's what."

Blunt took the simcortex and stuck it in her back, Betty White coming to life almost instantly.

"Where am I?" she said, her eyes trying to take in the people and the room, finally widening as she caught sight of the body on the table. "Oh, my, what has happened to Jimmy, my Mr. Potz?"

"Dead," said Grave. "We found him—and you—on the beach, near the conference center."

Betty looked puzzled, her eyes blinking rapidly. "That is not possible. The doctor's projection was seventeen more days, and he's usually spot on."

Grave frowned back at her. "I'm afraid he's been murdered, Ms. White."

She looked confused. "Ms. White? No, my name is Shirley."

"All right, *Shirley*, do you remember being at the conference center?"

Shirley slowly nodded. "Yes, Jimmy wanted to try out the new section of beach. We got there at 7:00 P.M. precisely, walked around, sat on the beach, and talked about life and death. When it started to get dark, we went back to the van. As I settled him in, he noticed we had forgotten the blanket, so I went back for it." She suddenly looked disoriented. "And the next thing I knew, I was here."

Sergeant Blunt stepped closer to her. "Was there anyone else in the van?"

Shirley looked around, trying to figure out where the voice was coming from. "Who said that?"

"Over here," said Blunt.

She zeroed in on the sound, finally taking in the vague shape of a man to her right. "Ah, there you are. Yes, well, there should have been someone else—Jimmy, our new driver—but he wasn't in the driver's seat, as he should have been. We were so long on the beach, he probably wandered off for food, or um, you know."

"So he was human," said Blunt.

"Yes, I think so."

"Could you describe him for us?"

Shirley frowned. "Not really. We were already in the back seat when he came and drove us to the beach."

"And you didn't see him?"

She shook her head. "No, there's a privacy barrier between the front driver seat and the back seats. All I know is he smelled of crab."

"Crab?"

"Yes."

Blunt rolled his eyes and nodded at Grave. "All yours, sir."

"Okay," said Grave. "Do you know the make and model of the van?"

"No, but it should be easy to identify. It's clearly marked as a Crab Cove Hospice Center van."

"Okay, great," said Captain Morgan, jumping in. "Now, what can you tell us about your patient, this Jimmy Potz?"

Shirley seemed relieved to talk about something she *did* know, her voice near monotone as she laid out her relationship to Potz. "Jimmy Potz, sixty-two, no relatives, shift foreman at Crab Cove Pick 'n Pack, on medical leave, terminal, inoperable brain tumor, loves jazz, puppies, and long walks on the beach."

"And how long have you been his hospice partner?"

"Three days, sixteen hours, four minutes."

Morgan was about to ask another question, but Grave jumped back in. "What can you tell us about that time period? Did you notice anything unusual?"

Shirley cocked her head. "Unusual?"

"You know, his mood, things he may have said, apprehension?"

Shirley shook her head. "He was pretty much textbook. Worked his way through the stages of grief to acceptance, and began to put things in order, preparing for his death—even visited two cemeteries yesterday to compare burial sites and costs."

"And you accompanied him to the cemeteries?"

"Yes, of course, although the officials at both graveyards insisted on speaking with Mr. Potz in private. I insisted back, of course. I'm not allowed to leave a patient's side, for any reason."

"And did this Jimmy person drive you there?"

"Yes."

"And you really never got a look at him?"

"No, sorry, I was focused on Mr. Potz."

"I see, and did Mr. Potz say anything after those visits?"

"Only that he was happy with his choice."

"And which did he choose."

"The new one, the Crab Cove Cinema Cemetery. He was happy, no *elated*, by the choice and wanted to take a walk on the beach to celebrate."

"And that's all you remember?"

"Yes."

"What about his medications?" asked Polk, stepping forward.

"Pretty standard. I have an array of injectables to handle mood, pain, any medical situation, really. And the van is stocked with all manner of drugs."

"And what did you inject during your time with him."

"Nothing."

Polk blinked. "Nothing? Isn't that unusual?"

Shirley shrugged. "Not really. He was early in the process, with seventeen days to go, and everyone has different reactions to pain and imminent death."

"I see." He turned to Grave. "Sorry to interrupt, Grave."

"Not at all."

Grave tried to think of something else to ask, but he didn't think they'd get much more out of Shirley, at least not without help from simdroid experts. "Shirley, thank you for your help."

Shirley smiled back, relieved. "Would someone take me to the hospice center, then? I am sure I must have a new patient waiting for me."

Grave looked at Morgan, who gave a little shake of his head.

"No, Shirley," said Grave. "I'm afraid we will need to keep you here, at least for a time." He motioned to Blunt, who pulled the simcortex out and eased Shirley into a nearby chair, a bewildered look frozen on her face.

"Well," said Captain Morgan, "at least we know who he is."

"Yes, that's a start," said Grave. "I'll head out to the Pick 'n Pack and see if there's anything there to go on."

"If I may, sir," said Bunt, "I'll take the simcortex out to Ramrod Robotics to have it examined. Perhaps it's been tampered with in some way. And we should at least have video of her movements."

Grave smiled at that. He knew Blunt, the nervous father-to-be, just wanted to check up on June.

Morgan seemed not to notice the hidden agenda. "Okay, what about the cemeteries?"

"I doubt we'll learn much there," said Grave, "but I'll swing by."

"Okay," said Morgan. "What about the van?"

"If you can locate it, I'll send my team out to have a look," said Polk.

"Great," said Morgan. "I'll send someone out to the conference center to check on the van and any security cameras covering the parking lot and the beach. So, anything else, Grave?"

"Jimmy, the driver. Where is he? Who is he?"

"Oh, right," said Morgan. "I'll get on the horn with the hospice center and see if we can track him down. Have we forgotten anything?

Grave shook his head.

"Okay, then, I need to get back to the station. Detective Snoot says she has a lead on Clink."

Grave looked surprised. "Really?"

"Yeah," said Morgan, turning to Polk. "And how about you? Are we done here?"

"Yes, except for the formal autopsy, but that is going to be pretty much pro forma. Toxicology will be the key this time."

"All right, then I guess we're done. How long before the results?"

"Should have the tox report later today. If anything else turns up, I'll give you a call."

"Good," said Morgan. "Okay, gentlemen, let's roll." He started to walk toward the door, then stopped and turned back to them. "Or in my case, let's hover," he said.

Blunt and Grave gave him quick, obligatory nods and smiles, recognizing that the captain drove a hovercraft these days, albeit an old, reconditioned one shipped to him from the NYPD, a police force that had made the transition to flying cars almost a decade ago. However clunky they were, hovercraft were considered state of the art, at least in Crab Cove, where most of the citizenry and the force drove old electric cars or, like Grave, long outdated cars with internal combustion engines.

They said their farewells and walked outside, each heading for different cars. Morgan stopped short when he saw Charlize, and gave Grave a disapproving grunt before walking away.

The hood to the Sprite was up, Charlize draped across one of the front fenders, fiddling with the engine. He sighed at the sight of her perfect body. Maybe she was right about his condition.

7

The Crab Cove Pick 'n Pack, a long, steel-sided warehouse, was ringed on three sides by a wide pier swarming with men, women, and simdroids unloading bushels of crabs from half a dozen crab boats, some rigged for nets and some rigged for trotlines. Crab pots were stacked everywhere along the pier, as were the heavy dredges the crabbers would use in winter months, when crabs went dormant and burrowed into the sea bottom.

On the land side of the building, refrigerated trucks were being loaded with bushels of live crabs and boiled crabs destined for restaurants, as well as containers of picked crab meat headed for distribution centers across the state and the country. The whole area smelled of crabs, some fresher than others.

Charlize drove the Sprite slowly by the trucks, and pulled into the only visitor parking space, the sound of gospel music abruptly replaced by the sound of screaming gulls as she turned off the engine.

"Come along," said Grave, "Record everything, and feel free to ask questions."

Charlize beamed. "Yes, sir."

They got out of the car and walked into the employee entrance, where they were greeted by an elderly receptionist behind a glass wall, whose eyes went wide when Grave flashed his badge.

"Oh, my," she said, "how can I help you?"

Grave put his badge away. "We'd like to talk to the manager."

"That would be Mr. Finn. May I say why you're here?"

"No, I'd rather you didn't, but it is a matter of some importance and urgency."

"I see," she said, moving to an intercom and paging Mr. Finn, the sound of her voice echoing throughout the plant.

Minutes later, a large man in a white lab coat and black rubber apron pushed into the reception area, his hand extended toward Grave, his eyes focused elsewhere, on Charlize.

He was a head shorter than Grave, and bald, with shark-like dead eyes set wide above a large, broad nose topped by a hairy mole that wagged its antennae as he spoke. He smelled of crabs, of course, but who wouldn't after even a few minutes in this plant.

"Lester Finn," he said. "How can I help you?"

Grave flashed his badge again. "Detective Grave. We're here about Jimmy Potz."

Finn blanched. "He hasn't died already, has he?"

He seemed genuinely concerned.

"Yes, I'm afraid so."

Finn shook his head. "So soon? I thought he had more time."

"He should have, Mr. Finn, but he was killed, murdered."

Finn seemed shocked. "*What?* Who would do that? Everyone *loved* old Clawfinger."

"Clawfinger?"

"Yes, his nickname around here. He was the best, a legend, at least until the simdroids came along. No man can top them at picking and packing, let me tell you. Still, old Jimmy could hold his own pretty well, although he tired near the end. He was a good manager, too."

"So, no enemies, no one with grudges against him?"

Finn shook his head. "No, as I said, he was loved, universally *loved* around here."

Charlize stepped forward. "If I may, I have a question for you, Mr. Finn."

Finn eyed her appreciatively. "Sure, have at it, honey."

Charlized cringed at the *honey*. "Let's turn this around a bit. Did Mr. Potz have any grudges or conflicts with any of the other employees? Any of the simdroids?"

Finn sighed. "Against employees, no. As for the simdroids, he was annoyed by, even jealous of, their skills. Frankly, every man and woman back there has similar concerns."

"For their jobs?"

"Yes."

"I see," she said. "Now, as to the conflicts. Was it general, or was it focused on one particular simdroid?"

Finn paused and stroked his chin. "No, not really, and it wasn't exactly conflicts. More like grumbling, mostly in the locker room, away from the droids."

Charlize turned to Grave. "Anything else, sir?"

"Yes," said Grave. "I wonder if we might take a look at the production line."

"Sure," said Finn, "although we'll have to suit you up. Hygiene is a big thing here. You could operate on our picking tables."

Finn gave them lab coats and masks and aprons and escorted them through the plant, from the industrial-sized cookers, to the flash-freezing machines, to the picking and packing stations.

When they reached the picking station, Grave stopped in his tracks. Along with six humans, there was an equal number of simdroids, and they all looked like actor Peter O'Toole. Seeing them brought back memories of the Hawthorne mansion, which employed eleven of them, all Peter O'Tooles. The only way to tell them apart was their unique voices, the voices of old twentieth-century actors. His favorite, Smithers the butler, had the unmistakable voice of Richard Burton and had helped him with the investigation.

Mr. Finn noted Grave's reaction. "Disconcerting aren't they. Picked them up for a song at a yard sale at the Hawthorne mansion. They're old models, of course, nothing like the sophistication of your, um, partner here, but cheap is cheap. All I had to do was get them reprogrammed for picking, and that was that."

"Did they say why they were selling them?"

"Bad memories, they said."

Grave looked back at the pickers. It was easy to discern who was a human and who was a simdroid, even apart from all the simdroids looking like Peter O'Toole. They were just plain faster, their hands as blurry as the cloud that was Sergeant Blunt.

"When did this happen?"

"About two months ago, just before Jimmy got his diagnosis and retired."

"Interesting. Can I assume that six humans lost their jobs here at about the same time?"

Finn gave him a sheepish look. "Yes, a couple of weeks later."

"And who let them go, you or Mr. Potz?"

"Potz. I thought it would go over better if he did it. The workers loved him, you see."

"And did it?"

Finn frowned. "No, it was pretty nasty all around."

"So *universally loved* Mr. Potz now had six people angry at him." *And I have six new suspects*, thought Grave.

"Yes, I guess you could say that."

"We'll need their contact information."

"Of course, you can pick that up from Sookie on your way out."

Grave turned to go. "Oh, one other thing. By any chance does one of your simdroids have the voice of Richard Burton?"

Finn shook his head. "No, someone else must have bought that one."

"They sold them all?"

"As I understand it, yes. I got the last six, or so they told me."

"I see. Well, thank you for your time, Mr. Finn. We may have additional questions at some point, so don't be surprised if we return."

"Not a problem," said Finn, offering his hand.

Grave shook Finn's hand and motioned a disconcerted Charlize toward the door.

Where are you, Smithers? he thought.

His phone began to ring. *Dad, dad, dad.*

8

Charlize set upon him as soon as they were out the door. "Simon, we need to interview the current employees and get access to the simcortexes of those droids. Their video recordings might give us a better sense of the interactions between the droids and the humans, Jimmy Potz specifically."

The Peter O'Tooles had so startled him, the thought never came into his head. "Damn, you're right."

"Shall we go back in?"

Grave checked his watch, which read 45:17. *Damned watch!* He fumbled with the buttons, finally figuring out the correct sequence to display the actual time, which was 11:32 a.m. "No, I want to get you back home and drive over to my father's place."

"I could come along."

"No, I'd rather you didn't." Grave had told his father about Charlize, but didn't want to expose her to his womanizer of a father. Since Grave's mother had died, Jacob Grave had become amazingly randy for a septuagenarian, at least for a few minutes a day.

"As you wish, sir. I can use the time to work on my plans for the car."

"Plans? What do you mean, plans?"

Charlize paused. She had discussed this with him before, but now it seemed even more urgent. "We received another price increase notice from the gasoline dealer. The costs of running this car are skyrocketing. We've reached the tipping point where it would be cheaper to just pull the engine and put in an electric motor."

Grave had resisted the change before, hoping to keep the car pristine as a way to honor his father's gift to him, but the costs were just climbing too rapidly, and his father didn't seem to care one way or the other. "All right, I guess there's no way of avoiding it."

Charlize actually giggled, although it sounded more like a child's giggle than an adult's. It was the kind of giggle that would burst from a child being tickled. "Great! I've had my eye on a Teslamatic 7500, state of the art. The batteries would fit in your hand, and—

"Later, Charlize, later."

Charlize stopped her giggling, but couldn't resist smiling. "Yes, sir. I'll have the plans ready for you upon your return."

"Good."

"But what about the simdroids, sir?"

"That can wait for now. I'll have someone swing by and do a memory dump on all of them. And we can interview the humans tomorrow. Come on, I'll drive."

Grave slid into the driver's seat and watched as Charlize slid into the passenger seat, her long legs bent provocatively at the knee, which accented the curve of her thighs.

His deep sigh was lost in the sound of gospel music as he started the car and pulled out of the parking lot. The music lasted for only a few minutes, and then Reverend Bendigo Bottoms came on to offer his commandment of the day.

"I love that song, don't you?" intoned the reverend, his voice a deep basso. "Now, my commandment of the day goes back to Exodus 20:4, 'Thou shalt not make unto thee any graven image, or any likeness of any thing that is in heaven above, or that is in the earth beneath, or that is in the water under the earth.'

"Now, the last time I looked, crabs are something in the water under the earth. Oh, yes, they are. You know it, you all know it. And you probably know what I'm referring to here. That's right, those paintings of crabs, in purple no less, that litter the shops and walls of this town. The worship of crabs in this town has been bad enough, but now—*now!*—we have to deal with these paintings wherever we go. Why, there's six of them on the walls of every Skunk 'n Donuts in town. Crabs doing this, crabs doing that. And I say, enough of this idolatry. Take these graven images down!"

After a brief pause, the gospel music resumed. Grave knew exactly what the reverend was talking about. The death of artist Whitney Waters, famous for her stylized paintings of red herrings, which technically were actually red mackerels, had left a void of sorts in the Crab Cove art world. After her murder in the Hawthorne mansion, her paintings, which were ubiquitous about town, became too valuable to display.

A new artist, Pinky Bloom, had quickly filled the void, her paintings of purple crabs filling the walls and adorning the windows of homes and shops throughout Crab Cove and the Greater Crabopolis. Merchandise soon followed, from mugs to keychains, to garden flags, to bumper stickers, to mailboxes, to "I survived the Crabopolis" tee shirts. Even Charlize had one, which she wore when she tuned up the Sprite.

They rode on in anything but silence, the sound of gospel music signaling their approach to pedestrians, who invariably covered their ears and scurried into shops to get away from the noise. Grave sometimes thought of his car as a boon to local businesses. He wondered how many people had actually bought something after he and the gospel Sprite had chased them inside.

Minutes later Grave pulled into the driveway and watched as Charlize extricated herself from the Sprite. Maybe she *was* too beautiful for him.

She smiled at him. "Okay, don't forget. Tonight, the plans!"

"Of course." He backed the car out of the drive and sped away, covering the distance to his father's house in less than a single gospel song.

His father was on the front porch, waiting for him in a suit and tie, which was beyond odd. His father hadn't been out of his stained pajamas in weeks.

9

Simon Grave walked up the porch steps, his father silently ushering him in through the front door. When he stepped inside, he gasped. The usual mess and clutter had been replaced with what actually looked like the inside of a well-tended home.

"What in the world?"

Jacob Grave chortled. "I thought that would be your reaction. Had it cleaned up."

Simon gave him an appraising look. In his experience, there was only one thing that could promote tidiness in his father, and that was a new case. But since his father had retired years ago, it could only be an old case, and that could only be one specific case.

"You're not working on the Clink case again, are you?"

His father smiled. "I am, and I'm making progress, believe it or not. Working with a psychic, perhaps you've heard of her. Ida Notion."

"A notion about what?"

"No, that's her name. *Ida Notion.*"

Simon snorted. "You're kidding?"

"Not at all, but here, have a seat. That's not why I summoned you."

Jacob Grave pointed at his plastic-covered recliner, his favorite chair. "Here, sit."

Simon sat down reluctantly, the plastic crinkling around him, and looked up at his father, who hovered over him, a withered old bald man in a suit that seemed to consume him.

At 72, the once tall and robust man had become withered and hunched, with rod-thin legs that could barely support him. His hair, once thick and black and wavy like Simon's, had left him entirely, revealing a head that resembled a honeydew melon with ice blue eyes. Simon shuddered every time he looked at him. Is *this* how he would look one day?

"Now," said his father. "First off, I want you to know that I'm *fine* with it. I've *accepted* it." He waved his arms at the clean room. "And this cleaning is part of it."

Simon leaned forward. "Part of *what*, dad? What are you talking about?"

His father sighed. "I'll get right to the point. I have stage four pancreatic cancer. I'm going to die, Simon."

Simon felt flushed and dizzy. "Wh-what?"

"Now, now, calm yourself. We all have to die of something, and this is the hand I've been dealt."

Simon stood up and grabbed his father's shoulders. "Are you sure? Did you get a second opinion?"

His father shrugged him off. "No need, Simon. I've trusted Doctor Zorn all these years, and I'm sure he's right."

Simon cringed at the mentioning of Doctor Zorn, a doctor well into his seventies and far removed from medical progress.

"But—"

"No buts."

"But I thought the cancer vaccine covered that."

His father rolled his eyes. "No, it covers everything *but* pancreatic and brain cancers. Just my luck."

"But—"

His father gave him an exasperated look. "Stop with the buts! I can't negotiate my way out of this. I'm a dead man walking, and that's that."

Simon tried to focus. "So what is the treatment plan, and the prognosis?"

"Three months tops without treatment, six with."

"And the treatment?"

His father shook his head. "I'm going to forgo treatment. What's the point? And don't tell me three months is three months. I just won't go through the agony of treatment. I need to stay sharp, or as sharp as I can be, if I'm going to catch Chester Clink, which I assure you, I have every intention of doing."

Simon dropped back into the chair, trying to come to grips with the situation. He knew arguing with his father was useless. The man was just too stubborn. Perhaps he could have a talk with Doctor Zorn, get copies of the test results, and consult a specialist.

"All right," he said finally, and as calmly as he could muster. "How can I help?"

"With the case, nothing. But I do need your help with one little detail."

Simon frowned. "Yes?"

"Doctor Zorn encouraged me to put my life in order, including selecting a funeral home and cemetery. The funeral home is a given. We'll use Wiggins. They did right by your mother, made her look twenty years younger. And besides, I've always liked the look of their hoverhearses."

"And you'll want to be buried alongside her, of course, in the Crab Cove Garden Cemetery."

His father frowned and threw up his hands. "I'm not sure. You know how I hate the plastic flowers they use to mark the graves."

"Yes, but mother's there, after all."

His father held his hands up in front of Simon in a way that suggested he was worried that Simon would suddenly leap up at him. "Now, Simon, don't you go getting upset, but I'm thinking of using that new cemetery just outside of town. Doctor Zorn gave me a brochure, and it seems quite exciting."

Simon couldn't believe his ears. "*Exciting?* You're going to be dead, dad. And what about mom?"

His father began pacing back and forth in front of him. "Now don't you go worrying about *her*. We'll move her. There's a special discount for relocations."

"A discount?"

"Yes."

Simon threw up his hands. "Oh, the wonders of afterlife marketing."

"Simon, don't be cute. I need your help checking them out."

Simon sighed, then nodded. "Well, dad, as it turns out, I need to go there today as well, for a new case."

"You don't say?"

"Yes, so if you're ready, we can head over there now."

His father shook his head. "No, too early. I had a call with the director there, a Mr. Winter, and he encouraged me to come about half an hour before sunset, so I could get a full appreciation of the cemetery's benefits. And he didn't want me to miss the fireworks."

"Fireworks?"

"Yes, fireworks. Here, take this brochure along with you and pick me up about eight. Can you do that?"

Simon took the brochure, which looked like a gaudy, full-color advertisement for a theme park. And perhaps it was. "Of course."

10

Grave's first impulse was to go home and take some time to digest the news of his father's imminent death, but the thing about Grave was that he only found peace and solace through work.

He tossed the cemetery brochure on the passenger seat without looking at it and started up the car, the gospel music taking on a wholly different meaning as he weaved his way through traffic, seemingly on automatic pilot, his thoughts elsewhere as the car took it upon its Spritely self to deliver him to the visitor parking lot of the Crab Cove Garden Cemetery, Crab Cove's oldest cemetery and now a competitor of the Crab Cove Cinema Cemetery, or C4, as the brochure emphasized in large, bold type on its cover.

He wondered briefly whether the other C4, the Crab Cove Conference on Crime, knew about this apparent violation of its trademark. That thought led to a brief courtroom scene in his head, with the cemetery's defense attorney arguing the salient points in the case as the conference's attorney objected time and time again. In the end, which came quickly, Grave realized he didn't know a thing about trademarks.

Case dismissed.

He got out of the car and stared out across a field of gravestones, each sporting bouquets of plastic flowers, some in gaudy colors no flower had ever achieved. Several of the nearby graves seemed new, the dirt still in mounds, the gravestones pristine. A hundred yards away, a backhoe was busy digging a new grave. He knew from experience that the new grave was not far from his mother's. Perhaps today would be a good time to visit.

He turned and headed into the office building, a low brick building shaped exactly like a brick, but with windows. Walking into the foyer was like walking into a scented-candle store, the atmosphere cloyingly sweet.

The receptionist seemed to be elsewhere, so he rang the little bell on the counter and waited.

Moments later, a tall, thin man dressed in a dark blue suit came striding down the hall, a smile growing on his face in a way that suggested a long-practiced approach, step one of his multistep plan to get new business. He was hollow-cheeked and wan, with deep pocks on his face indicating a struggle with severe acne as a teenager. His pencil-thin red moustache, a match for the thick, neatly combed hair on his head, twitched and danced as he struggled to maintain the smile. Grave could tell he was sizing him up, the man's milky green eyes seemingly scanning him from head to foot.

Step two, offering his hand in greeting, was in progress as he launched into step three, a warm though solemn greeting designed to give the grieving some confidence that all would be well, or at least as well as could be expected. "Welcome to the Garden," he said. His voice was surprisingly high, almost a squeak, like a false note from a piccolo.

Grave took his hand, which was as cold as, well, the grave, or a hand that seemed to have been kept in the freezer waiting for just this occasion. "Thank you," said Grave, flashing his badge with his other hand.

The badge completely shattered the man's countenance, which switched from business-like warmth to a dark, frowning place where snakes and many-legged insects dwelled. "How can I help you, detective? We don't often see police here, I mean, other than for a funeral service."

Grave put his badge away. "Sorry, "I didn't mean to startle you, Mister..."

"Smith, James Smith. I'm the director here."

"Great, you're just who I wanted to see."

Smith held up his hand and motioned toward a nearby doorway. "Well, then, shall we go to my office?"

Grave nodded, Smith directing him a little ways down the hall and into a large office that shouted opulence, from its mahogany desk to its plush gold velvet chairs to its matching silk-threaded wallpaper. It was like walking into a gilded trap.

Smith motioned him into a chair in front of his desk, and then took the position of power behind the desk in a tufted, tall-backed leather chair that screamed executive dominance.

Smith rocked back in the chair. "Now, then, how can I help you?"

Grave cleared his throat. "There's been a murder."

Smith's eyes grew wide, but Grave could not be sure whether the reaction was one of surprise or just greed for new business. "And how do we fit in?"

"You don't really, but the victim, a Mr. Jimmy Potz, was said to visit here yesterday morning."

"Potz, Potz," said Smith, shuffling through papers on the corner of his desk. "Ah, here we are. Yes, another terminally ill person scouting out his last resting place."

"And did he make a decision?"

Smith slumped back into his chair. "Yes, but not in our favor. He was persuaded to go with C4. Have you heard of them?"

"Yes, the new cemetery across town."

Smith's lips curled in disgust. "They're absolutely *killing* us."

"Business down, is it?"

"No," said Smith, leaning forward. "Just the opposite—what with our aging population, people are dying left and right—but C4 is getting the bulk of the business, at least from the terminally ill. We have four new graves out there, and need to dig three more today, but C4 must have three times that."

"I see. So, getting back to Mr. Potz. What was his mood?"

Smith sighed. It was clear he wanted to rail on about C4, but relented. "He was in a good place. Calm. Seemed to be fully in charge of his faculties. Certainly didn't look like he was about to drop dead, even given his age. But he had one of those hospice droids with him—looked just like Betty White, if you can believe it—and that doesn't happen without a death sentence."

"No, of course not. Tell me, was the meeting unusual in any way? Things he might have said, for example."

Smith pursed his lips. "Nothing *unusual* about what he said—he pretty much kept to the details of burial—but as to the meeting itself, yes and no."

"Oh, how so?"

Smith rocked back, lacing his fingers together in front of him. "Mostly, I deal with relatives of an already deceased person. But lately, it seems to have flipped to meeting with people who are about to die, and they're a much harder sell. They're not grieving, you see. Not in a hurry to get past a sad event."

"Are they mostly old people?"

Smith shook his head. "No, all ages, especially this time of year: drunk driving, drunk swimming, dearly departed surfers, also drunk, not to mention other traffic fatalities, pedestrians and so on. But, to your point, a good number of old people, many with terminal illnesses. Makes you wonder if there's something in Crab Cove's air or water, or *something.*"

Indeed, thought Grave. With the exception of a few exotic diseases and heart conditions, most of the major diseases had been cured, including most cancers, diabetes, Parkinson's, and a host of other maladies and syndromes. Life expectancy was soaring. The topic of the day was not death, but how to deal with the benefits and problems of a population that refused to die, in an era when robots were taking over the workplace.

Grave nodded. "It does seem odd." He stood and offered his hand across the desk to Smith, who seemed to be relieved that the meeting was over. "I'll be on my way, then."

Smith shook Grave's hand and then stepped out from behind the desk. "Please feel free to let me know if you have further questions."

"Thank you, I appreciate that."

Smith led Grave out of the office and down the hall, but parted ways with him to greet a couple clearly in the throes of grief. Grave walked outside and scanned the graveyard. The backhoe had moved to another location and was hard at work digging yet another hole.

Grave glanced at his watch, which thankfully and unusually gave him the correct time: 2:15 P.M. He still had plenty of time before he needed to pick up his father, so he decided to head back to the station and check in with Blunt and Morgan, and perhaps Polk.

He nodded in the direction of his mother's grave. "Sorry, mom, another time."

11

On a whim, Grave decided to take the scenic route to the station, pulling off the main highway and taking the coast road along the bluffs of Crab Cove, which had become somewhat less scenic over the last ten years as island after island succumbed to the water rise of global warming. Smith, Deal, and Tangier Islands, islands he had visited and played on as a boy, were now lost forever, their populations dispersed, many opting for lives in Crab Cove, which itself would become an island in an estimated fifty years. And who knew how long even that would last.

The turnoff back to the highway came all too quickly, Grave downshifting to slow the car and merge with the traffic, which was heavy as usual for an August day, the town knee-deep in tourists trying to make the best of a vacation before their children had to return to school. Five minutes later, he was pushing into the lobby of the station, which was also busy. Muggings, assaults, domestic disputes, beach violations, traffic violations, and a panoply of other diversions from the law were in full display. Officers, including a dozen summer deputies, moved people about or clacked on keyboards to bring each arrest to a formal conclusion or dispensation.

The coffee pot was empty, as usual, as was the box of donuts, which Grave knew from experience was a swift event, the chocolate donuts disappearing first, followed by glazed, cinnamon, jelly, cruller, and finally plain, the last donut disappearing in sections as officer after officer refused to take the last donut, at least in whole.

He could see Captain Morgan in his glass bubble of an office, seemingly talking to himself. He had to squint to make out Sergeant Blunt, who was having a bad visibility day.

Grave rapped gently on the door and walked in, Morgan swiveling in his chair to greet him. "About time, where have you been?"

"Working, of course. Paid a visit to Pick 'n Pack and the garden cemetery. Seems our Mr. Potz fired six workers not long before his death, so we could be looking at a revenge killing."

"We'll need to bring them in," said Morgan.

"Yes, of course, and we'll have to interview the current employees. We'll also have to copy the memory banks of the six simdroids who replaced the dismissed workers. Their videos might reveal something."

Morgan looked startled. Grave could tell from the look that Morgan shared his concern that simdroids might be involved in the killing, just as they had been in the Hawthorne mansion murders.

Morgan recovered quickly. "Oh, right. Well then, I'll get on that and have the videos sent over to Ramrod. Blunt, you can take the lead on reviewing them. Anything else?"

Grave chuckled. "The funniest thing. You'll appreciate this, too, Blunt. The simdroids were six of the *Hawthorne* simdroids."

"Wow," said Blunt, his voice coming from an unexpected direction. "I'd heard about them selling the droids off, but I didn't know where they ended up."

"And who knows where the other five are? I really wonder who got Smithers."

Morgan rapped his knuckles on the desk. "Can we stick to the case?"

Grave nodded. "Of course, sir."

"So," said Morgan, raising his eyebrows, "anything else?"

"Not much. I went to the Crab Cove Garden Cemetery and interviewed its director. Potz had visited, but apparently was not impressed. Decided to be buried at the new one, the Crab Cove

Cinema Cemetery. I'm heading out there later this evening for a look-see."

Morgan turned to Blunt. "Okay, Blunt, bring him up to speed on the simcortex."

"Right, sir. I took the simcortex to Ramrod Robotics and viewed Shirley's video for the last day of the victim's life. It's as she said. She took him to the van, seat-belted him in, looked into the front seat—no Jimmy—looked around briefly, and then walked back for the blanket, which is where the video ended, of course."

"What about the van," said Grave, "did we find it?"

"Yes," said Morgan. "Forensics is on it."

"And the security cameras?"

Morgan sighed. "The conference center is new, as you know. The cameras have not yet been installed."

"Crap," said Grave.

"Yeah, tell me about it," said Morgan.

"What about the driver, this Jimmy person?"

"Ah," said Morgan. "A further mystery. Seems the hospice center has never even heard of him."

The three of them sat there in silence for a few minutes, trying to piece together the puzzle, Morgan rocking his chair back and forth and Blunt doing whatever a cloud does in silence.

"So," said Grave, finally, "any word from Polk?"

"Oh, of course," said Morgan. "Toxicology is back. Seems the murderer used chloroform to subdue Potz, then gave him a series of three shots."

Morgan picked up the report from his desk. "Let's see. Yes, according to Polk, Potz was administered a fairly standard cocktail of drugs used in executions and in euthanasia."

"Wow," said Grave.

"Indeed. Here you go. The first shot was pentobarbital, which means he was unconscious in less than thirty seconds. Of course, he was *already* unconscious from the chloroform, so the first shot was probably unnecessary. In any event, that was followed by pancuronium bromide to stop breathing, and then potassium chloride to stop the heart."

Grave knitted his brows. "So the murderer sees Shirley headed back to the beach, puts Potz under with chloroform, and then disables Shirley before returning to administer the fatal injections."

"That's pretty much it," said Morgan.

"Did Polk say how long it would take to administer the shots?"

"He thought at least ten minutes. There has to be time between the shots, otherwise they'll interact too much, whatever that means. Polk was not specific." He rolled his eyes. "As usual."

"It sounds like a medical professional, someone who knew about the drugs and how they worked, and knew how to give an injection."

Morgan frowned. "That was my first thought, too. But Polk says the injections were pretty amateurish, and remember, the first shot was overkill—he was already unconscious."

"What a cluster," said Blunt. "No video of the murder, and a murderer who had his way for ten minutes or more. Surely there must be a witness, given the number of people at the conference."

"You would think," said Morgan.

"Wait," said Blunt. "It's a *paid* parking lot."

"So?" said Grave.

Morgan perked up. "The attendant!"

"What attendant?" said Grave. "I thought they were all computerized these days."

"Not all," said Blunt. "Fancier places like the conference center prefer to have real humans. Kind of a throwback thing."

"Really?" said Grave.

"Yes," said Blunt. "And he or she might remember the comings and goings. There might even be time-stamped evidence, even a credit card transaction."

"And with any luck," said Grave, "the attendant might be a simdroid."

"And then we'd have video, maybe even sound," said Blunt.

Morgan slapped his hand on the desk. "Great! Head on over there, Blunt, and see what you can find out."

"Yes, sir." Blunt floated toward the door.

"Wait," said Grave, "I'll go with you."

"No," said Morgan. "I need to talk to you about another matter. Go on, Blunt, you're losin' daylight."

Sergeant Blunt floated out the door, then disappeared completely, a cloud on a mission.

Morgan turned to Grave. "Now, Grave, this business about your father."

Grave seemed shocked. "How could you know? I just found out myself."

Morgan gave him a puzzled, incredulous look. "What are you talking about? You know I know your father is up to his old meddling on the Clink case."

"Oh, that," said Grave, relieved that he didn't have to share his news with Morgan, at least not yet.

"Yes, *that*. Detective Snoot says he's been up to his old tricks again. Interviewing witnesses and stickin' his nose into the investigation. Hell, he's even workin' with a psychic."

"Ida Notion," said Grave, absently.

"What, you *know* about this?"

"No, I mean yes, I mean I just found out about it."

Morgan fumed. "Well, I want you to have a talk with him—a *firm* talk—otherwise I'll be slapping him in jail for interference with a police investigation."

Grave sighed. "I'm seeing him this evening. I'll handle it."

Grave knew that would not go well.

12

Charlize greeted him at the door with a glass of wine, which he declined. "Thanks, but I have some driving to do tonight. Have to check out the Crab Cove Cinema Cemetery."

She squinted at him. "What's wrong, you seem down."

Grave walked past her into the living room and slumped down on the couch. "It's about my father."

He told her everything, which somehow made him feel better. Her empathy programming was exceptional. The way she looked at him, the softness of her voice, the light touch of her hand, all put him at ease and gave him confidence that he would get through this. She also knew that work was his go-to response to stress of any kind.

"You'll be fine," she said, giving him a comforting but firm pat on his hand. "Now, tell me about the case. Where are we?"

Grave smiled weakly at her. "You know me so well."

Charlize smiled and gave a little confirming nod of her head.

"Okay, then," said Grave. "Here's what we know."

He rambled on for several minutes, Charlize nodding thoughtfully with every new piece of evidence—or lack of evidence—and then he stopped. "So, that's about it."

Charlize closed her eyes, which Grave knew was part and parcel to her way of processing data, and sat in silence for several minutes, finally opening her eyes. "A couple of things," she said, launching right in. "The missing driver, Jimmy."

"Yes?"

She pulled a piece of paper out of her pocket. "That whole thing about the driver, Jimmy, smelling of crab. There are two Jimmies on the list of fired employees. Jimmy Notch and Jimmy Dibbs. We have their contact information, so that's something we can pursue."

"Of course, the crab smell." He checked his watch. "I have to leave soon, so we can pick up on this tomorrow."

"Will I be able to come?"

"Yes, absolutely."

She smiled broadly. "One other thing, Simon."

"Yes."

"The number of people dying, it's going way up, especially in the last few months. I checked old issues of *The Claw and Mallet*, and it's astonishing. The obits run to two and three pages now."

"Interesting, and you think..."

Charlize sighed. "I think perhaps we are dealing with more murders than we realize."

"Another serial killer?"

"Maybe."

Grave nodded slowly. "Yeah, but then again, we have an aging population. Maybe it's to be expected."

Charlize shook her head. "Statistics suggest otherwise. And just think about it. We called Potz's death suspicious only because we found him on the beach with a disabled simdroid. What about people who may have died in bed or under less suspicious circumstances?"

"Okay, we'll have to check the records. Hospitals, funeral homes, relatives."

"That's my thought as well."

Grave puffed out a sigh. "A lot of work."

"Yes, but work is just what you need. Now, run off and shower. You smell like a crab baking in the sun."

Grave laughed and sniffed at himself. "Oh, my, you're right."

He stood and started to leave the room, but then turned back. "Oh, we were going to talk about your plan for the Sprite."

She shrugged. "It can wait."

"No, you do what needs to be done. Just don't touch the radio."

Charlize screamed with delight. "Yes!"

He waggled his finger at her. "Again, just don't touch the radio."

She rolled her eyes. "Oh, Simon, you and that radio. Can I at least put in a toggle switch to mute it when necessary?"

Simon crossed his arms. "No, I don't think so."

"Simon, Simon, a *toggle switch*. It's so British, so Spritely. They come in all colors now. It would be so sporty."

Simon loved a good toggle switch, it was true, but he loved the loud, uncontrollable sound of gospel music even more. And besides, he didn't want anything more in his life that would bring back his old habit of speaking with a British accent. He had been accent free for six months, and didn't want to risk it. "Um, no."

"Think about it."

His thoughts were already elsewhere, back on the case.

13

Simon knew the evening would be a solemn affair, so he dressed counterintuitively, in white Bermuda shorts and a bold Hawaiian shirt filled with parrots and palm fronds, an outfit that would have delighted Lola. Death might be coming, but not without a little pushback *joie de vivre* from the living.

His father greeted him at the door, wearing what might be his death suit, an out-of-date gray suit with lapels large enough to serve as wings on a windy day. He looked Simon up and down, trying to grasp what his son might be thinking.

"Simon, you realize we're going to a cemetery, right?"

"Yes, of course."

His father shrugged. "Suit yourself. Come on in, I want you to meet someone."

Simon stepped in the door, immediately catching sight of a small woman sitting behind his father's card table, which was filled with stacks of folders Simon knew were related to the Chester Clink case. She had her tiny hands resting palms down on the files as if the words within were being drawn into her.

She was not dressed like a gypsy, which is how Simon always imagined psychics would dress, but wore a powder blue pants suit accented by a flowered yellow scarf tied tightly around her neck, no doubt to hide wrinkles. Her dark brown hair was pulled back into a tight bun, which emphasized her round, moonlike face and large golden eyes topped by penciled-in, inverted v-shaped brows that gave her an ever-surprised aspect. A nose that would have made an eagle proud carved her face in two, resting just above large, puffy lips painted scarlet. Simon couldn't help thinking that the inspiration for her face must have been a Mr. Potato Head set.

"Simon, may I introduce Ida Notion, the psychic that's helping me on the Clink case."

Simon crossed the room and shook her hand. "A pleasure to meet you."

She pursed her lips and squinted at him. "You are not lucky in love." Her voice was deeper than Simon expected.

"What?"

"It's in your eyes. A sadness. A loved one has moved away. Very distant, I think."

"Um, yes, that's right." His father must have told her about his breakup, if you could call it that, with Lola LaFarge. Grave thought of it more as a disappearance.

She smiled, cocking her head to one side, her eyebrows raised in victory. "Your father tells me you have no faith in people like me."

Simon shrugged. "It's not about faith. I've just never seen a case *solved* by a psychic that couldn't have been pieced together from the available evidence."

Notion shrugged back, harder. "We shall see."

Simon turned to his father. "Dad, I think we should be going."

His father glanced at his watch. "Yes, sorry. Ida, I'm afraid we'll have to pick this up in the morning."

Ida stood and made ready to go, although she was not much taller standing than sitting. "Not a problem, Jacob. But give some thought to what I've said. I keep getting the image of a white van, and I think that's important. It's dark, and it's pulling off the road and into a field. One headlight is out. It's missing a hubcap on the left front wheel. There's a sign on its side, but I can't quite make out the words."

Simon's father looked up at him, beaming. "See, we're on to something."

"Apparently," said Simon.

14

Barry Blunt, detective sergeant and cloud extraordinaire, pulled into the driveway and floated into his house, where he found his equally nondescript wife, June Thursday, bent over the sink, washing dishes. When she saw him—and she could actually see him, unlike most people—she turned off the faucet, wiped her hands on her apron, and gave her watermelon of a stomach a gentle pat.

"How was your day, dear?" she said, waddling to the kitchen table and sitting down.

"Long," said Barry, sitting down opposite her. "Sorry to be late, but I had to interview a parking lot attendant."

"About that murder?"

"Yes, I was hoping he would have seen something, perhaps the killer, but he wasn't exactly Mr. Observant. Said he only remembered people's hands and the bills or credit cards they held in them."

"What about transaction records? You know, credit cards and such."

Barry sighed. "Not much help. The machine was down, so he was only taking cash."

"Who uses cash anymore?"

"I know. He said he was turning people away."

"What about time stamps?"

"Same deal. Nothing much. Six cars went in and five cars went out during the time period, but Mr. Observant couldn't match them to the time stamps, or remember anything about them.

"Wait, what about security cameras?"

"Nope. Hadn't been installed yet."

"Oh, dear."

"Very frustrating."

"So where does that leave you?"

Barry cataloged the evidence and the steps they were taking to move forward.

"I had a thought," she said when he finished. "About the simdroid, you know, Shirley."

"What about her?"

"Her recorders were set for video only, which of course is the default setting. Audio is such a battery drain."

"So?"

"So, perhaps she heard something, or perhaps we should review the video from days ago, when she first met this Mr. Potz."

Barry smiled at her. "You know, you really should consider joining the force. You'd make a great detective. Really, your talents are wasted at Ramrod Robotics."

June patted her tummy. "Well, that's kind of you, sir, but I have other business in mind, at least for now."

Barry chuckled. "Right. Anyway, Shirley is still at the morgue. I'll reanimate her tomorrow morning, and see if there's more to learn."

"Good, I'll try to find out more about her specific model. Swing by Ramrod when you're finished. We can view the video in more depth, too. "

"Sounds like a plan. Oh, and we'll have more video to review from the six simdroids at Pick 'n Pack."

"What, more simdroids?"

"Yes. Oh, and you'll love this, they're the same simdroids from the Hawthorne mansion."

June perked up. "Really?"

"Yes, although I'm not sure which six simidroids."

June chuckled. "Well, this should be fun, don't you think?"

"Yes."

They grew silent, Blunt ruminating on tomorrow's plan, June watching her husband's ruminations, which went on far too long for her to stand. She decided to change the subject.

"Barry, how's Detective Grave doing?"

"Doing?"

"I mean, without Lola."

Barry shook his head. "He seems distracted, out of focus. Sometimes he just seems *elsewhere*."

"Do you think that new simdroid of his has anything to do with it? I thought for sure he would pick out a petite brunette to remind him of Lola, but he went just the opposite, a tall beautiful blonde."

Barry shrugged. "Dunno. He seems pleased with her, especially her mechanical skills."

"Time will tell, I guess."

Barry wasn't so sure. In his experience, Detective Grave had a hard time approaching women. As Grave had told him many times, he didn't know how to make the pitch, let alone close the sale. "Yes, I guess."

They fell silent once more, June ruminating on the Simon-Charlize relationship, and Barry watching his wife's ruminations, which went on far too long for him to stand. He decided to change the subject.

"So, are we having dinner?"

June snapped out of it. "Oh, yes, meatloaf. Should be ready soon."

Barry smiled broadly. Put him on a deserted island and his only request would be for meatloaf—and June, of course. He couldn't even boil water. "Great."

June picked up her chair and moved it closer to Barry's, ready to change the subject once again. "Well, then, enough about Grave and detective work—and meatloaf. Time to return to our favorite subject."

Baby names, thought Barry. They were having a hard time coming up with baby names that fit their families' long-held naming conventions, primarily because June had decided to keep her maiden name, Thursday. Blunt's family scheme was alliteration, so his father was Bixby and his brothers were Barnaby, Baxter, and Bart. Thursday's family, on the other hand, named their children for months of the year, consistent with their birth month, thus June Thursday and her sisters May and April.

Barry groaned. "You mean *your* favorite subject."

"Now, Barry, naming a baby is important. Hear me out."

"All right," he sighed.

"Now, there's no question the baby will be born in August, so I propose August and Augustina."

"But those are A names. We need a B name."

"Exactly, so how about August Benjamin Blunt or Augustina Beth Blunt?"

"No, the B has to come first. It would have to be Benjamin August Blunt or Beth Augustina Blunt."

"That could work, I guess, but you win and I lose."

"And I don't much like Benjamin or Beth, to be honest."

They fell silent, June drumming her fingers on the table, Barry looking at the ceiling.

"Okay," said June, finally. What if we changed things up a bit, go with a hyphenated last name?"

"Blunt-Thursday?"

"Or Thursday-Blunt."

"I don't know. Let's think about it a little more, okay?"

June grabbed her stomach, Exhibit A in her argument. "Barry, we're running out of time. I'm about to *pop.*"

"Don't worry, we'll think of something," said Barry. He sniffed the air. "Is that meatloaf I smell?"

"Oh, no!" June shouted, standing and rushing to the oven.

She opened the oven door and a third cloud entered the room, one redolent of burnt meat.

15

The difference between the Crab Cove Cinema Cemetery and the Crab Cove Garden Cemetery could not have been more striking. Instead of traditional headstones and garish plastic flowers, the new cemetery featured brushed stainless steel obelisks topped by video monitors of various sizes. Not a single flower, real or otherwise, was in evidence.

"Is this for real?" said Grave, looking out over the cemetery.

"Pretty cool, huh?" said his father, walking away from him. "Come on, we're keeping Mr. Winter waiting."

Grave turned and followed his father up the sidewalk to the visitor center, a large silver dome that looked like it would be more at home at the new Mars settlement. A tall, white-haired man in a white suit and tie stood in the doorway, beckoning them with a rosewood cane topped by a gleaming silver knob the size of a tennis ball. His hair was pulled back into a tight ponytail that appeared off-white next to his brilliant white suit. He had dark eyes, a large, broad nose, and lips so large they seemed cosmetically enhanced. They seemed to vibrate as he spoke, each word accompanied by a low hum, as if he were talking through a kazoo.

"This way, the show is about to begin." With that, the man turned and walked inside, leading them down a short hallway to a theater already packed with people.

The man pulled a sheet of paper out of his pocket and glanced quickly at it. "You're in seats 6A and 6B, to the left and up."

Grave and his father worked their way up the steps and slipped into their seats, the lights dimming briefly to indicate that the show was indeed about to begin.

The man in white walked to the center of a small stage, his back to a wall of video monitors. He tapped his cane three times on the floor.

"Good evening and welcome to C4, your path to everlasting life after death. As many of you already know, my name is James Winter, and I am the director of C4. Tonight, think of me as your guide to the afterlife. Here, you will find no granite stones, no flowers, no signs of mourning whatsoever. No place to be buried and forgotten. No place to celebrate death. If that's what you want, leave now. I'm sure the garden cemetery can find a hole for your body and any bouquet of plastic flowers your heart desires."

He paused, scanning the room. Nobody moved.

"Good. You've all received brochures outlining the range of our après-death benefits. Think of it as a menu. Select the features you like. Build your own package. It's your afterlife, after all."

Several people in the crowd laughed, and Mr. Winter smiled back at them.

"I see some of you have a good sense of humor about this. Good, you can express that humor—or any emotion you wish—right here at C4, where our goal is to celebrate you, your life, your achievements— the you *you* want people to remember, forever."

He turned and pointed at the video monitors with his cane. "It's a simple concept, really. Your life in living color on a monitor however big you want, broadcasting your life in whatever manner you wish, with any message you wish. We'll work with you and your loved ones to create just the right video homage."

A bald man in the first row raised his hand.

"I see you have a question," said Mr. Winter. "Let me guess, if I may. You are wondering about cost."

The man nodded and lowered his hand.

"Well, here's the good news. Depending on the package you select, the cost could be a little or a lot or even *zero*. And you might even *make* some money. As the brochure describes, we are partnering with PostTube, the leading website for honoring the dead with obits, life summaries, and related celebratory videos. They'll be working with us to help create your lifestream videos, which will be featured here and on PostTube. And if you opt in to the advertising program, you could create a revenue stream for your family."

Several people thrust their arms in the air.

Winter chuckled. "Now, now, I know you have questions, lots of questions, so my staff docents will be available immediately after this presentation, both here in the building and out along the paths throughout the cemetery. They'll be easy to spot from their costumes. For now, sit back and enjoy the show. You'll be seeing representative videos, videos of real people who have chosen to live on with us here."

Without further ado, he tapped his cane once, hard, on the floor, and walked from the theater. The lights dimmed, and the video screens sprang to life.

The videos ranged from very simple photomontages to what looked like brief film trailers to longer, professionally produced and edited productions, complete with inter-spliced commercials.

The lights came up to a smattering of applause, and people began to work their way out of the theater. A dozen docents awaited them in the foyer, some dressed in white, others inexplicably dressed in period costumes that ranged over three centuries, to answer questions and hand out headphones for the walking tour.

His father tugged him down the hall, away from the crowd. "We have an appointment. Come on."

Mr. Winter was waiting for them in his office, which looked more like a control room. Winter sat at a console filled with buttons and switches, facing an array of monitors, each running a different video.

He spun around and motioned them into two white leather recliners, which whirred to life as soon as they sat down, positioning them so they could better view the video screens.

"So," said Winter, "what did you think?"

"Where do I sign?" said Grave's father with a chuckle.

"Whoa," said Grave, alarmed.

"Whoa nothing, this is *perfect.*"

Winter raised a hand. "No, your son is right. This is nothing to rush into. Remember, it's forever."

Grave's father shrugged. "Of course."

"Dad, can I at least ask some questions? This is a big decision."

"Whatever." His father crossed his arms and looked away.

Grave turned to Winter. "We have a couple of questions, one of which is cost and the other concerns my mom."

Winter nodded. "I know about your mother's situation. Yes, there will be a fee charged by the garden cemetery for her disinterment, but if you've read the brochure, you'll know we have a two-fer discount, which in effect means that her reburial will be free."

"Free?"

"Yes, unless of course, you opt for separate videos specific to her life as well."

"I see, so if Dad decides to have one video for the both of them..."

"There's only one fee, which of course will vary depending on the options you select. And if you select one of our partner funeral homes and/or ministers, you'll receive additional discounts."

"Tell me about the advertising."

"Yeah," said his father, "tell us about that. I think that's the way I'll want to go."

"It's pretty simple, really. First off, your video would be posted on PostTube and would feature a range of 30-second advertising spots. The more people that like or follow your video, the more ad revenue you'll receive."

"Works for me," said his father.

"But what about here at the gravesite? Are you saying there would be commercials playing on his screen out there?"

"It's an option, and one I would highly recommend."

"And would we have the right to refuse certain advertisers?"

"Not specific advertisers, but you could opt out of certain *categories* of advertisers, say, ads for guns, liquor, or porn."

His father brightened. "You have ads for porn?"

Winter chuckled. "Of course. Pretty much anything you can imagine."

"Well," said Grave, "what about—?

Winter interrupted him. "I think everything will be made clear when you take the tour. Talk to the docents out there. Then, if you have further questions, we can meet again."

Grave sighed. "All right, we'll take the tour and get back to you."

"Good, be sure to use the headphones and the remote, so you can hear the videos and vote on them."

"Vote?" said Grave's father.

"Yes, if you like the video, press like. The more likes your video gets, the more revenue you receive from advertisers, and you earn frequent viewer points for additional discounts and rebates."

"Okay," said Grave. "One of the reasons I came here tonight is to ask questions about a Mr. Potz, who recently signed with you, I believe." Grave pulled out his badge.

Winter was taken aback. "Police?"

"Yes, I'm investigating the murder of Mr. Potz, and would like to ask you a few questions."

Winter threw up his hands. "Whatever you want, officer. But can we do that in the morning? My schedule is pretty full tonight."

"As you wish," said Grave. "How about ten tomorrow."

Winter pulled out his phone and checked his schedule. "How about 10:30? That will give us plenty of time to discuss Mr. Potz and any other questions you may have about our services."

"That works," said Grave. "Come on, dad, let's take a stroll through this *wonderland*."

The sun had set by the time they made it outside, the whole cemetery now alive with hundreds of monitors broadcasting the lives of strangers. Then the fireworks began.

"Holy shit," said his father, which pretty much summed it up.

16

The Crab Cove Cinema Cemetery sat there in the morning mist, a ghost of what Grave had seen the previous night, a riot of videos celebrating the lives of the famous and not-so-famous residents of Crab Cove. Graveyards are otherworldly in the first place, but C4 was setting a new standard for over-the-top otherworldly.

Grave had walked alongside his father, who seemed delighted by every video presentation, from fade-in, fade-out simple photographs of the deceased's life to computer-enhanced extravaganzas. Two of the presentations, for the victims of The Hawthorne Mansion Murders, Epiphany Jones and Whitney Waters, had sent chills up Grave's spine. It was beyond disconcerting to see the two women, lovers in life and both beautiful in their own ways, smiling out at him, Epiphany giving people a tour of her art gallery, and Whitney painting red mackerels in the nude, as was her custom. They were so alive, and yet, so completely dead.

Some of the gravesites were so popular, they attracted large crowds. Grave could just make out brief images of beautiful people doing beautiful things, the crowds cheering at times, then growing silent as commercials interrupted the videos. Grave wasn't at all sure commercials were the right way to go, but his father grew more and more insistent as they made their way through the cemetery, the path doubling back to the visitor center, where they handed in their headphones and remotes, and headed home, the ear-shattering gospel choir putting an end note on the evening.

Grave had been eager to interview Mr. Winter, so he had left home early the next morning, arriving at the cemetery a good half hour before the scheduled appointment. The thick fog that usually accompanied a summer morning in Crab Cove had resolved into a mist that was burning away rapidly, revealing more and more monitor-topped obelisks, as well as a few people strolling through the cemetery.

He decided to follow their lead and tour the grounds, just to see what they were like in daylight, when the screens went black and silence ruled. As he walked along, he could see a young girl up ahead seated on a bench and looking like she came from another century. *A docent*, he thought.

The closer he got, the broader her smile became. She couldn't have been more than ten or eleven years old, with red hair and freckles that made her seem even younger. She was dressed in a simple gingham dress that seemed to shout eighteenth century. She seemed very shy.

"Good morning," he said, his voice seeming to startle her.

She seemed delighted to see him. "Oh," she said, "good morrow to you as well."

Grave smiled at her choice of words. *So docentish.* "May I join you?"

She smiled up at him and slid to the right, making room for him. "Yes, please do."

Grave sat down and stared out at the cemetery. "Quite a place."

"Indeed," said the girl, placing her hands in her lap.

"What can you tell me about it?"

She seemed puzzled. "I don't know. What would you like to know?"

Grave shrugged. "Anything at all. My father is thinking about this as his final resting place."

"Oh, how wonderful," she said, beaming. "We will certainly welcome him with open arms."

Grave frowned. "Frankly, I'm not completely sold on the place. What do you think of these videos?"

"Oh, they're not so bad, once you get used to them, although it makes for a long night. That's why I prefer the day shift. It's just more peaceful."

Grave nodded. "I'm with you on that." He looked at her dress. "So, why the old-fashioned dress? I thought this was a fairly new cemetery."

The girl looked down at her dress. "Oh, this. I see what you're saying, but no, this is a very *old* cemetery, or at least one section of it is."

"Oh?"

She nodded vigorously. "This used to be the Skunkford Cemetery, a plot initially reserved for members of the Skunkford family. Dates back to the mid-1700s, when the town was founded."

The town itself, as Grave well knew, had been called Skunkford, after its founder, Sir William Skunkford, whose family had settled the town in 1750 with a modest land grant from the king. The good people of Skunkford had changed the name of the town shortly after the American Revolution, the name, "Little Willie's Landing," chosen to disparage Mr. Skunkford's legendary anatomical shortcoming as payback for his support of the crown, as well as to encourage his rapid flight. Centuries later, a developer had changed the town's name yet again to attract tourists interested in crabs.

"You don't say."

"Yes, truly."

Grave smiled at her. "Well, that explains the dress, then."

She looked down at her dress again. "What? I don't follow."

"You know, now it makes sense to me, is all."

"Oh, I see," she said with a quick smile.

"So," said Grave. "Do you get many questions on a typical day?"

She moved her head from side to side, giving the question proper thought. "A good number. Most just want to know more about the cemetery. Some are put off by it, of course. And still others are just in a state of shock over the whole prospect of death and graves and cemeteries."

"I would expect so."

"Indeed."

"All those questions must be tiresome for you, I expect."

She shook her head vigorously. "Oh, no, it's my job as greeter to answer every question, however difficult. It's just what I do, you see."

"Yes," said Grave, "yes." He slapped his hands on his thighs and stood. "Well, then, I best be on my way. Thank you for the pleasant conversation."

"It was my pleasure."

Grave turned to walk away, then turned back. "Oh, may I ask your name? I'll put in a good word for you with the management."

"Um, Victoria."

"Very good. Well, then, *Victoria*, goodbye for now."

"Goodbye, sir, please come again."

He nodded and walked away, picking up the pace in order to make it back to the visitor center for his appointment. A whirring sound made him look up. A drone was busy writing a message in the sky: *RIP Jimmy.*

Grave didn't wait for the drone to finish its work.

17

Sergeant Blunt arrived at the morgue shortly after ten and said his hellos to Polk, who was busy with another autopsy, and Detective Amanda Snoot, who hovered near Polk. Neither of them returned his hello, which was pretty much par for the course with those two, friendliness being far down the attribute scale for both of them.

The arrival of Snoot and her grim aspect at the precinct had put a pall over the place. She was always the first to arrive in the morning, some thought to claim the only chocolate donut, but most thought to work some spell to drain morale.

Everything about her was pinched. When she looked at you, she squinted in a way that suggested you were some low, barely sentient entity not worthy of her presence. Her one patented response to everything, good or bad, was to screw up her tiny mouth in lemon-sucking disdain. Thin as a rail with a head too large for her body, she looked like a walking doorknob, a doorknob with rust-colored short hair cut both long and short, as if she had been sheared this way and that by a mischievous child.

Blunt shuddered at the sight of her and went to the far side of the examination room, where the inanimate Shirley was propped against the wall. He slid the simcortex into her back, and she bubbled to life, muttering gibberish until her systems took hold and actual sentences came out.

"Oh, my, am I still here?" she said, looking around.

"Yes," said Blunt, "but not for long. Come along with me."

Shirley looked left and right. "Who's speaking?"

"Me."

Shirley tracked the voice and squinted at the blur beside her. "Oh, you, the cloud-man."

Blunt sighed. "Yes, come along."

Shirley adjusted her skirt and walked with Blunt out of the examination room, down the hall, and into a small office, where Blunt knew they could talk in private.

He motioned her into a chair. "Have a seat, this won't take long."

She sat down and gave him her best look of concern. "I need to get back to the center."

"Soon."

"They will miss me."

Blunt held up a hand. "Yes, I know, and the faster we do this, the faster you will be back at work."

"Good," she said, sitting back and smiling.

Blunt took out his notebook. "Now, I'd like you to think back about the day of the murder. We've looked at your videos, but of course, there's no sound to go along with it."

"No, that is by request only."

"Exactly, now firstly, what did you discuss on the drive from the center to the beach?"

Shirley cocked her head, a programmed response, indicating that data was being sorted. "He wanted to know all the details of euthanasia. How it was done, what was involved."

"And what exactly did you tell him?"

"That it was easy-peasy, that we had all the meds we needed right there in the van should he decide to go that way."

"Really? Is that encouraged?"

Shirley shook her head. "The time and manner of death is up to the patient. We are there to ease them into it, however they decide to go."

"So the meds were in the van?"

"Yes, and I told him the exact sequence I would use—and their effects—if ever he should choose that option."

"And do you think your driver, this Jimmy person, could have heard you?"

"Oh, yes. Although I couldn't see him, there is an open mic, just in case I needed him quickly."

"I see. So, you were with him for about three days. Did anything else happen during that period that gave you concern or seemed odd?"

"Nothing unusual. Like all my patients, there is a period of time where they express their anger."

"And what was Mr. Potz angry about?"

"Simdroids, for one. Taking jobs at the plant. But mostly he was angry at Mr. Finn, his boss, for making him fire six employees."

"I see. And did he discuss any of that on your ride from the center to the beach that day?"

"No, as I've said, it was mostly about euthanasia."

Blunt closed his notebook. "Okay, Shirley, I think that's all I need for now, but don't be surprised if you see me again over the next few days. I may have more questions."

Shirley brightened. "So, we're done?"

"Yes, come along, let's get you back to the center."

Blunt took her by the arm and escorted her out of the morgue and into his squad car.

"Oh, my, I've never been in a police car."

"It's not all that."

"Can we run the siren and flash the lights?"

"Um, no."

He started the car and pulled out of the parking lot. He did not see Polk racing after him, trying to get his attention.

18

Mr. Winter stared back at Detective Grave as if he were not quite sure how to answer the question or how best to avoid answering.

"It's a simple question," said Grave after some moments had passed in awkward silence. "What can you tell me about Mr. Potz?"

Winter cleared his throat as a way to delay further. "Yes, *simple*. I was just trying to figure out where to begin."

Grave raised his eyebrows. "You know what they say."

Winter leaned forward in his chair. "Yes, all right, I had an appointment with him and his simdroid a few days ago. We discussed C4, just as I had discussed C4 with you and your father. He was excited and pleased, and signed up on the spot."

"What kind of package did he get?"

Mr. Winter spun in his chair and plucked a file folder from a rack behind him. "Here we go. Let's see, let's see. Oh, yes, he signed up for one of our deluxe packages—large monitors, tall obelisk, custom videos, advertising, the works."

"Can I ask the price?"

Winter pursed his lips, which seemed reluctant to spit out a price.

"Please," said Grave, "it could be important."

Winter sighed. "Oh, very well, the package came to $37,500."

Grave was taken aback. "So much? For a crab picker?"

Winter didn't seem shocked at all. "He said he had no relatives, so why not go whole hog? Or words to that effect."

"I see, and how do the payments work? I mean, he's dead now. How do you get your money?"

Mr. Winter rubbed his hands together in a way that suggested he was delighted with his money-making scheme. His voice took on a conspiratorial tone. "Half is paid up front, to cover production expenses and the like. The rest is guaranteed to us through a codicil to the person's will." He sat back, thoroughly pleased with himself.

"*Will?* Why would a crab picker have a will?"

"He didn't, but our legal team provided all the necessary paperwork. All we need now is to have his body delivered to our partner funeral home, Satin Passages."

Grave wondered at the name. *Why is death so full of euphemisms? Why not a funeral home that tells it like it is? Dead Body Depot or Carl's Cadaver Center or something.*

"I don't recall that one," said Grave. "Is it new?"

"Yes, just opened a few months ago. We have a small stake in it."

"I see. Well, as for the body, that will take a few more days, I'm sure. Autopsy, evidence, and so forth."

"We are very patient, detective. Waiting is part of what we do. In the meantime, we are crafting the video according to his instructions."

"May I ask what that will be?"

"Certainly. He gave us some raw footage of a crab-picking competition he won a few years back. He thought it would soon be a lost art now that droids are getting into the business. We'll throw in some historical footage on crabbing, as well as news footage on the competition, and that should do it. Oh, and Pinky Bloom, the artist, has bought advertising to sell some of her crab tee-shirts."

Well, of course she did, thought Grave. "Interesting, but tell me, what was his mood when you met with him?"

Winter smiled. "As strange as this might seem, detective, he was cheerful, happy to get on with it. Like so many of our clients."

"It?"

"Death, and his legacy video. He was ready to go."

And go he went, thought Grave. "One more question, Mr. Winter. In your meeting, did the simdroid Shirley take part in any way? Did she say anything?"

Winter frowned. "Yes, she kept referring to herself as the voice of reason, cautioning him about spending so much and so soon, when he clearly had many more days to live. And so on."

"I see."

Winter waved a hand in front of himself as if he were politely dismissing a fly. "It's her programming, I don't fault her for that. And he was quite insistent, so she eventually backed off."

"And you closed the deal."

Winter smiled smugly. "Oh, yeah."

Grave closed his notebook and stood. "Well, then, I think I have all I need for now."

Winter stood and shook Grave's hand. "If I can be of further help, just let me know."

Grave suddenly remembered his conversation with Charlize about the increased number of deaths.

"Oh, as a matter of fact, I *do* have another question. How is business? I mean, overall?"

Winter seemed delighted by the question. "You saw the crowd last night. Business is good, *very* good."

"Have you noticed an increase in business over the past few months?"

Winter stroked his chin. "Not particularly."

"Really?"

"Nothing unusual in the overall numbers. We're killing the garden cemetery, is all. More people coming to us, and you can certainly see why."

Grave nodded politely. "And the usual mix of deaths—accidents, illness, drownings, and the like?"

Winter shrugged. "Pretty much. This *murder*, of course, is quite unusual, apart from the Clink victims—we have forty-five of them, you know. Oh, and those poor young women done in at the Hawthorne mansion."

Winter checked his watch. "And now, if we're done here, I have an appointment with a backhoe salesman. We can barely keep up."

Indeed, thought Grave. Then he thought of the docent.

"Oh, one last thing. I want to tell you how impressed I was by one of your employees, a young docent."

"Oh, who?"

"Victoria. I met her out on the path and we had a delightful conversation about the cemetery."

Winter seemed puzzled. "Victoria, Victoria, I don't recall a Victoria, but thank you. We're growing so fast it's hard to keep up with the junior staff. I'll be sure to let her know about your kind words."

Grave smiled, shook Winter's hand once more, and left the building. The sunny morning had turned into a gray overcast day, the kind of weather a cemetery should enjoy. The drone skywriter's message had long resolved to nothing, leaving the open question, *Jimmy who?*

He scanned the graveyard. A man in orange overalls caught his attention. He was leaning on a shovel at a new gravesite just up the path. Grave checked his watch, which continued to report the accurate time, and decided he had time to talk to the man. He strode the hundred steps to the open grave and pulled out his badge.

"Good morning, I'm Detective Grave. Can I ask you a few questions?"

The man gave him a why-me look, tentatively offered his hand, then pulled back. "Sorry, gloves are pretty dirty."

"No problem, and don't worry, this isn't about you."

"Why would I be worried? All I do is dig holes, morning till night, and sometimes *through* the night."

Grave admired the man's physique, which had been sculpted by the digging, and made a note to resume his gym membership. The man was easily in his sixties, but he could probably break Grave in half with his pinky. He was bald except for white wisps of hair that he had attempted to comb over without success. They stood and flapped in the wind like a tattered sail. His features were rounded, as if his maker had used a bowling ball as a model for his head. Blue-gray eyes set wide under bushy white brows gave him a gnome-like aspect, which was only enhanced by a large triangular nose, his nostrils sporting a forest of long hairs that waved and danced as he breathed. It looked like he hadn't shaved in several days, but the growth had not yet approximated a beard.

"I just have a few questions about the cemetery," said Grave.

"Well, not too many, I hope. I have holes to dig."

"Just a few minutes is all I need."

The man leaned harder on his shovel. "Okay, shoot."

"First, can I ask your name?"

"Sure, Eddie Sparks."

"And how long have you worked here, Mr. Sparks?"

Sparks stroked his chin. "Let me see. I think going on twelve years now. Of course, ten of those years it was the Skunkford Cemetery."

"So the new owners kept you on?"

Sparks shrugged. "Obviously. They knew a good worker when they saw one."

Grave looked around. "Are you the only gravedigger here?"

Sparks pulled out a dirty handkerchief and wiped his brow. "No, there are a couple of others, but they're slow and don't know how to dig a proper hole. Dimensions, you see, the proper clearances for the casket, the evenness of the walls, the depth. It all has to be just right."

"Right. I bet you're really looking forward to the backhoes Mr. Winter is buying."

Sparks gave him an alarmed look. "*Backhoes?* He said that? He said he was buying backhoes?"

"Um, sorry, I thought you would know. He's meeting with a salesman right now."

Sparks gave an angry glance at the visitor center, and spat. "You don't say? A fine mess that will be. A backhoe is fast, I'll give you that, but it's like using a mallet to cut a cake."

Grave tried to turn the conversation in a less stressful direction for Mr. Sparks. "So, have you noticed a dramatic increase in business, you know, holes?"

Sparks spat again and kicked a little dirt into the open grave. "A lot of dying. A lot. Hard to keep up." He shook his head. "Shit, *backhoes?"*

Grave tried to keep him on track. "But an increase, right?"

"Damned right," said Sparks. "The past few months, especially. People are dropping like flies, I tell you."

Grave paused and looked out over the expanse of the cemetery and its now dark, monitor-topped obelisks. "So what do you think of this cemetery, the monitors and all?"

"I think it *shits,* is what. A cemetery should be a place of mourning and peace, not some sideshow of graven images. It's idolatry to me, raising yourself up in celebration in the eyes of the Lord." He spat again for emphasis.

"Right," said Grave, nodding. "It is a bit much."

"Much? *Much?* It's sacrilege, pure and simple."

Grave looked down at the hole. "And who's this grave for?"

Sparks didn't hesitate. "Jimmy something. He's going to die in his bath."

Grave was stunned. "Going to?"

Sparks nodded once, hard, making it clear that he was certain. "Yes, I can't make out why. It's a little fuzzy, but I see him in water."

Grave's eyebrows were at full attention. "So you see things *in advance?"*

"Of course. Otherwise, how would I ever keep up?"

19

Sergeant Barry Blunt and his wife, June, sat in front of a bank of monitors in a control room at Ramrod Robotics. They had once again gone over the downloaded video from Shirley's data banks, but had made little progress, save for their progress through a box of donuts from Skunk 'n Donuts, the local donut shop. One donut remained, the shop's signature Little Willy Cruller, named and sized to ridicule a diminutive body part of the town's founder, William Skunkford.

June pointed at the cruller. "Would you like that?"

"No, go ahead."

She snatched it and dispatched it with the skill of a woman in her final days of pregnancy. She had gained thirty pounds, but to Barry she was still the most beautiful woman in the world, albeit a woman as nondescript as he was, the two of them barely visible to the rest of the world. If ever two people were meant for each other, it was Barry and June.

Barry started to stand. "So, are we done here?"

June pulled him back down into his chair. "No, I want you to look at the very end of the video again, where Shirley is walking toward the blanket on the beach. I saw something that concerned me that last time through."

"What?"

"Just wait." She fiddled with the dials and switches on the console and the video fast-forwarded to the very end. Then she backed it up to show Shirley's final steps. They could see her approach the blanket and look out over the bay, gulls flying back and forth and skimming over the tops of the waves. Then a blur came across the screen, and the video ended.

Barry gave her a questioning look. "What? I didn't see anything."

She rolled the video back and played it again, pointing at the blur that briefly filled the screen. "That."

"The blur?"

"Yes, I think it's her left arm, reaching back."

He looked at the blur again, and it remained a blur. "So?"

"So it could be important."

Barry stared at her, waiting.

"Let me explain," she said.

"Please do."

"Shirley is an older model. When Hawthorne came up with the idea of the simcortex, he didn't think it completely through, placing it within reach of the simdroid."

"I don't understand."

June gave him an exasperated look. "Barry, she could have *pulled out* her own simcortex."

"Interesting, but we found the simcortex out in the bay. When she pulled it out, she would have immediately gone inactive, right?"

"No, not at all. She would have still had the residual energy to throw it. One final act before she lost power entirely."

"The blur."

"Yes."

"Why would she do that?"

June raised her eyebrows, waiting for Barry to catch up to the *a-ha!* moment.

Finally, his eyes went wide. "So *she* could have killed Mr. Potz."

June groaned. "No, silly, we would have seen that on the video."

"Oh, right. Then *what?*"

"She could have *helped.*"

Barry looked baffled. "I don't get it."

"Oh, Barry, sometimes I really wonder about you. Think about it.

The murderer could have directed her toward the blanket, so the murder would not show up on her video."

"And hers were the only footprints."

"Exactly."

Barry shook his head. "That's certainly one possibility, but suppose—just suppose, mind—that the blur is in fact her left arm, and—"

June interrupted. "It *is*. It's plain as day."

"It's a blur, June." He held up a hand to stop her from interrupting. "But let's say it is her arm. If she retained some power after the simcortex was removed, couldn't the movement of her arm just signal that she had become aware that someone was pulling it out and reached back to stop them?"

June opened her mouth, started to speak, then stopped.

"That's *also* a possibility, right?" he said.

She puffed out a heavy sigh. "Yes, that's possible."

Barry stood up. "In either case, we need to let Grave and Morgan know. Come on, let's go."

"The station?"

"Yes."

"What about the other videos from the simdroids at Pick 'n Pack? We haven't touched them."

"They'll have to wait. Besides, I need a break, and I'm hungry."

June beamed. "Can we stop at Skunk 'n Donuts on the way? I'm famished, too."

Barry smiled at her and gave her a hug. "Of course."

They floated from the room, down the hall, and out into the gloomy day, two clouds among many.

20

After wrestling with the convertible top to the Austin Healy Sprite, Grave slipped into the car, turned the key in the ignition, and launched himself and the radio's gospel choir out of the parking lot and onto the highway, the sound so loud with the roof on that Grave's teeth vibrated and tingled.

Seconds later the choir abruptly stopped, and the deep, sonorous voice of the Reverend Bendigo Bottoms came on, offering up his commandment of the day, in this case, THOU SHALT NOT INVOKE THE DEVIL.

"As many of my parishioners know, I have occasion from time to inevitable time to offer condolences and sermons to those who grieve at funeral homes and cemeteries. But what did I see on my most recent visit to the Satin Passages Funeral Home? Listeners, you would not believe it—I did not believe it—but it is nevertheless true that someone, some miscreant, a teenager surely, had defiled that place of holy transcendence, oh yes he had. Workmen will no doubt erase this sinner's evil act, but it shall remain burned into my very soul.

"And what was it that he had done, you ask? What had he written that has so upset the Reverend Bottoms? I will tell you. With four strokes of a brush, he crossed out the "I" in satin and added an "A." Four little strokes was all it took to turn satin, a word that invokes a smooth lustrous fabric, the kind of fabric you would want to have around you as you went from this world to the next, to the vile word

"Satan," a blasphemous act that mocks the Lord and the recently deceased.

"Brothers and sisters, if this was the only such act I have seen in our fair town, I could dismiss it. But no, it has become all too common. We defile the houses of the Lord and our very graves. Stay tuned now for eight uninterrupted gospel songs. And while you listen, think about what I have said, and get ready for my next commandment, which will focus on a particular cemetery gaining popularity in our town. Until then, may God bless you all."

After a brief pause, the gospel music resumed, the fabric top to the car pulsing from the noise. Fortunately, the reverend's words had taken him from the cemetery to his father's house, Grave barely aware that he had driven the car at all.

Another car was parked in front of his father's house, and judging from its custom license plate—*SYKIK*—Grave could only deduce with a cringe that his father's psychic, Ida Notion, must be in the house. He extricated himself from the Sprite, a difficult process for a man so large in a car so small, but through practice he had learned to do it in a way that didn't suggest wrestling or climbing out of a deep hole.

He knocked gently on the door and let himself in, the smell of pizza and mold greeting him long before he laid eyes on his father and Ida Notion at the card table his father used as a desk. He may have cleaned, but the odors lingered like guests who've overstayed their welcome.

"Jesus," said his father, "you scared the crap out of me. Next time knock."

"I did knock."

Grave's father threw up his hands. "Whatever. Get over here. We were just discussing Clink's latest murder."

"The Bryson girl?"

"Exactly," said Ida. "I have a feeling."

"A notion?" said Grave, smiling at his play on words.

Ida shook her head dismissively. "I guess I should have expected that from you, but shall we turn away from your puerile amusement to the case at hand?"

His father grabbed him by the arm. "Wait till you hear this."

Grave pulled away. "Dad, you know you're not supposed to be doing this. This is Detective *Snoot's* case."

"Snoot? To hell with that sourpuss."

"Dad."

"Don't *dad* me. Listen to what Ida has to say."

Grave turned to Ida. "All right, what is this *feeling* you have, Ms. Notion?"

She smirked. *"Ida,"* she said.

"As you wish, *Ida.* Now, what do you have?"

She took a deep breath. "A feeling, as I've said, a feeling about our Chester Clink and how he goes about his murders."

"And what exactly is that?"

"I see him coming out of a house, or at least a building—I can't really see it or him—but through his eyes I can see the yard in front of him as he walks down the sidewalk and passes by a mailbox with a purple crab painted on it. He raps it with his knuckles. It's something he does before a kill."

"You mean one of those Pinky Bloom creations? Purple crabs this, purple crabs that, which she calls *art."*

Ida bristled. "She is a wonderful *artiste."*

Grave shrugged. "Well, that may be, but I hope you feel more than a Pinky Bloom mailbox. They're all over town. Even dad has one."

"No," said Ida, continuing her arched-back bristle. "This is an *original*, one of a kind, not those mass-produced ones you find in the gift shops."

"And what makes it unique?"

His father jumped in. "Red fish."

"Yes," said Ida, "an homage to the late artist Whitney Waters, famous for her stylized paintings of—"

"Fish," said Grave, completing her sentence.

"Red herrings," said Ida. "Little ones surrounding a large purple crab, its claws opened wide."

"Mackerels, actually," countered Grave. He could still remember how distraught Whitney had become when he pointed out the critical error she had made in attempting to paint a red herring, getting the dorsal fins all wrong for a herring but just right for a mackerel. Her explosive reaction had ultimately led to her death at the hands of a Hawthorne simdroid. "So, what else do you *feel?* I don't suppose you felt the house number on the mailbox."

"No, too fuzzy," she said.

"The mailbox is enough," said his father. "Find the mailbox, find Clink—game, set, match."

Grave struggled to set aside an image of his father playing tennis. "So you're just going to drive around town, looking for the mailbox?"

His father shrugged. "Yes, for a start. And we'll talk to the post office folks, of course. One of the carriers must remember that box."

Ida was shaking her head. "Jacob, why don't we just talk to Pinky Bloom? Perhaps she will remember who bought the mailbox."

Grave's father nodded in a way to suggest that he was about to say just that. "Of course, of course. Now, Simon, if you've nothing else, we'll be on our way."

Grave wanted to talk to his father about his prognosis and the decision about the cemetery, but not in front of Ida Notion. "No, by all means do your thing. Just try to stay out of the way of Detective Snoot. And be careful out there, dad. You're no spring chicken, you know."

His father frowned. "No, but this rooster isn't dead yet. And I'm going to get my man."

"Okay, dad, okay."

Ida picked up her purse from the table. "Ready when you are, Jacob."

"One more thing," said Grave. "If Clink has just knocked on his mailbox, doesn't that mean another murder is afoot?"

"Yes," said Ida. "So we need to work fast."

"But if you're a psychic, aren't you supposed to be able to see the future? Where the murder is to take place, and so on?"

Ida cocked her head, wondering at Grave's stupidity. "A common misperception. Some of us can, some of us can't. And, unfortunately, I can't. I see things that have already happened or are happening in the moment. I mean, I'm no Eddie Sparks."

Grave was both stunned and confused. "You know Eddie Sparks?"

Ida gave Grave a puzzled look. "Yes, I *did*, but how would you know the name?"

"I just talked to him."

Ida laughed dismissively. "That's impossible. No one has seen Eddie Sparks in a dozen years. He *completely* disappeared after the debacle of the Monroe killing."

"Yes," said his father. "He completely vanished. The press was all over him for failing to stop the murder."

The case was vaguely familiar to Grave, who was on the force then, but assigned to other duties. Sparks had apparently led police to the wrong location, and had fled in embarrassment. "Yes, I remember it now, but I know I met him at the cemetery this morning."

Grave described his encounter, Ida nodding vigorously at Grave's description of Sparks and his purported ability to see the future.

"It's him," she said. "Older now, of course, but definitely him." She turned to Grave's father. "We need to see him, now."

Grave suddenly remembered what Mr. Winter had said about the Clink murder victims: *We have forty-five of them.*

If Sparks could see the future, why in all those years did he not come forward about the Clink murders? He might have prevented all of them.

"You're right, we need to get over there," said Grave.

"We can take my car," said Ida.

"Right," said his father.

"I'll follow in the Sprite," said Grave.

They moved quickly out of the house and down the front steps to the sidewalk. Grave's phone began to ring, which he knew would be one of three people: Morgan, Blunt, or Polk. He hoped it wasn't Morgan, but his phone had other ideas. It *was* Morgan.

He swiped the phone's display and took the call. "Yes, sir."

"Grave, get your ass to the station, stat."

"But—"

"No buts except yours. I'm sittin' here with Blunt, and he and Polk have information that changes *everything.*"

Grave started to balk, but he knew he couldn't mention the Clink case. "Very well. I'll be there in ten." He hung up and turned to his father and Ida, who were opening the doors to her car.

"You guys go ahead. Something's come up. I'll join you later if I can. If not, please give me a call later."

"All right," said his father, climbing into Ida's car and slamming the door closed.

Grave watched them speed away. *Yes,* he thought, *everything is changing.*

21

As soon as he entered the station, Grave could see Captain Morgan talking to two clouds Grave took to be Barry and June in the Captain's fishbowl office at the back of the large, desk-filled room. Morgan spotted him and summoned him forward with his meaty hand.

Grave walked into the office and sat down next to Blunt. "Okay, what's up?"

Morgan sighed and began rocking in his chair. "A couple of things. Blunt, you go first."

The larger cloud began speaking. "I reviewed Shirley's video with June, and we think we've come up with an interesting alternative scenario." He paused.

"Go on," said Grave.

The smaller cloud jumped in. "It seems that Shirley's model has an interesting ability. She can reach her simcortex and extract it, and still retain enough power to fling it into the bay."

"Wow," said Grave. "So she could have been working with the killer?"

Blunt was quick to answer. "Or she was just reaching back, a reaction to sensing someone pulling it out."

Grave looked back and forth between Blunt and June and Morgan. "So how is that a case-changing revelation?"

"It's new *possibilities*," said Morgan. "New ways of looking at things."

Grave tried his best not to raise his eyebrows, but they had already rebelled. "Okay, in the first place, wouldn't that mean the killer would have to have some expert knowledge of simdroids? I mean, to direct her in that fashion, against her protocols to protect her patients?"

"That's what June and I think," said Blunt.

Grave moved on. "And no video of the driver?"

"No, just the name, *Jimmy*," said Blunt.

"What about the parking lot attendant."

"Nothing. Didn't see a thing."

"And the van?"

Morgan piped up. "Scores of prints to analyze, but no results yet."

"So we're still grasping at straws," said Grave. "I can't help wondering, why the beach, why the parking lot?"

"He must have seen it as his best opportunity," said Morgan.

"Or was in a hurry," said June.

"Or knew about the lack of security cameras," said Blunt.

Morgan turned to Grave. "So, were you able to talk to Jimmy Notch and Jimmy Dibbs?"

Grave shook his head. "No, but that's what I plan to do next. And I have to talk to the employees and simdroids at the Pick 'n Pack."

"And I'll be reviewing the simdroid videos with June," said Blunt.

"Sounds right," said Morgan, "but there's one more interesting thing. Polk completed his autopsy, and found something rather odd."

Grave leaned forward. "Like what?"

"Well, seems our Mr. Potz was in perfect health. No brain tumor at all."

Grave tried his best to analyze this new fact in light of the other evidence, but the only thing he could think of now was his father. *Is he really sick?* "Interesting."

Morgan raised his eyebrows. *"Interesting?* Is that all you've got?"

"For now, yes. Let me think about it. And in any case, it doesn't change the fact that he was murdered. Perhaps his diagnosis was based on a false-positive during testing."

Morgan was incredulous. "On a *brain tumor?* Is that possible?"

Grave shrugged. "I don't know. Do we know who his doctor was?"

Morgan picked up Polk's report. "A Doctor Zorn."

Grave noticeably flinched.

"What?" said Morgan.

"He's my *father's* doctor."

"So?"

Grave looked down at the floor and sighed.

"What?" said Morgan.

"My father. Seems Doctor Zorn says he has stage four pancreatic cancer. A death sentence."

"Jesus," said Morgan. "I'm sorry to hear that."

Morgan detested retired Detective Jacob Grave, but Grave could tell his words were sincere. There were no nuances about Captain Morgan. He said what he felt, and didn't pull punches, even when punches clearly needed to be pulled.

"Thanks," said Grave, "but now I have to wonder if the diagnosis is correct."

Morgan nodded solemnly. "I hope that's the case, for both your sakes, but what are the odds of two false positives?"

Grave sighed. "Yeah."

"On the other hand," Blunt began, hoping to add something significant to the investigation, but the hand was quickly cut off by Detective Snoot, who leaned into the room with a hand of her own, one that precluded other hands.

"We have a body," she said.

22

Grave could not remember leaving the station or climbing into the Sprite, but he was now well aware of the gospel music in his ears and the flashing lights of a dozen patrol cars in his rearview mirror, the sound of their sirens lost in the music as they made their way down Main Street, past Crab Corners, and onto Blue Crab Boulevard for the one-mile trip to Exit 16, which dumped the caravan at the gates of the Crab Cove Cinema Cemetery.

All Grave could think of was two words, *body* and *father*, and he hoped the two weren't connected. He pulled the Sprite to a stop, leaped out, and began running up a cemetery path, where he could see a patrolman, one of the Morgan Freeman simdroids, already stringing crime scene tape. Three other people stood within the yellow ring: his father, Ida Notion, and Pippa Wobbly, the reporter from *The Claw and Mallet*. He immediately had a sense of relief on seeing his father alive and well, mixed with a feeling of dread for the unavoidable confrontation between his father and Captain Morgan, and topped with a feeling of suspicion about the appearance of Ms. Wobbly at two consecutive murders. All these feelings merged to form a suspicious relief of dread that carried him under the tape and to the open grave where the others stood, looking down.

Grave peered into the Grave, then quickly backed away. "Holy shit, it's Eddie Sparks."

"Deader than dead," said his father.

Grave stepped to the edge of the grave again, and looked in. It was Sparks, all right. He was lying on his back, arms draped across his chest as if someone had taken the time to display him just so. "Do you think?" he said.

"Yes," said his father. "It's a Clinker."

"But he kills only young women," said Grave.

"Not anymore." His father stepped to the edge of the grave and began pointing. "Look, plain as day, deep knife wounds, Bowie knife for sure. It's him, all right."

Grave turned to Ms. Wobbly, who was standing on the opposite side of the grave, her arms across her chest, shivering.

"Why—how—are you here?"

She startled, as if waking from a dream. "Oh, it's you again," she said. "I, um, I was working on a story, the dramatic increase in deaths these past few weeks. I got here early for an interview with Mr. Winter. Thought I'd take a look around the cemetery, you know, for background." She pointed into the grave. "Found this—him."

Grave was about to ask another question, but the booming voice of Captain Morgan interrupted him.

"What in the hell are *you* doing here?" Morgan shouted at Jacob Grave. "And who's this?"

Jacob Grave bristled. "Conducting a *private* investigation is what I'm doing here, and *this* is Ida Notion, a talented psychic who is going to help me crack this case wide open, once and for all."

Morgan turned to Simon. "Get these people on the other side of the tape—*now!*—and keep them there."

Grave frowned and lifted the crime scene tape to allow his father, Notion, and Wobbly to scoot under, which they did reluctantly, his father whispering to him as he left. "I am going to solve this, so help me."

"Yes, dad, I'm sure you will," Grave whispered back. "Now stand aside for a few minutes. We'll need to talk with you."

His father nodded in the direction of Morgan. "I'm not talking to that bastard."

"No, of course not. Sergeant Blunt will take care of that."

His father offered one last disgusted grunt and moved away.

Grave turned back to the scene and Captain Morgan, who was looking into the grave, shaking his head.

"Looks like the work of Chester Clink," said Grave.

"It does, but Clink only kills young women. Or did. A copycat, maybe?"

"Could be, but this is definitely a man Clink would have liked to see dead."

"And why's that?"

"Don't you recognize him? It's Eddie Sparks."

The name startled Morgan. He looked into the grave again. "Holy crap, it is."

"I talked to him earlier today, right after I talked to Winter, the director here. I didn't realize it was him at first. The name just didn't register, and as you can see, he's changed physically over the past dozen years."

Morgan was mystified. "And why was Sparks even here?"

"He was a gravedigger, if you can believe it."

Morgan tried to get his head around that. "From renowned psychic to ditch digger. Well, I guess that's one way of disappearing." He looked over Grave's shoulder. "Here comes Polk, and maybe Blunt."

Grave turned and lifted the tape for them. "Body's in the grave."

Polk nodded and walked over to the edge. "Well, not much doubt about cause of death, I guess."

"No," said Morgan. "And take care with this one. It looks like the work of Clink, or maybe a copycat."

Polk grunted. "Not a woman, so probably a copycat. In any case, I'll know for sure once we get him back to the morgue. Did you find the weapon?"

"We just got here," said Grave, "but if it was Clink, we won't be finding anything."

"We'll comb the area anyway," said Morgan. He turned to where he thought Blunt was standing, and pointed down the hill, toward the patrol cars. "Blunt, get those officers working on that."

"Yes, sir," said Blunt, his voice coming from a wholly unexpected direction.

Morgan rolled his eyes. "One of these days I'm going to figure out where you are Blunt?"

"Yes, sir," came a voice that was clearly already yards away, far down the hill.

Grave pulled his phone out and began tapping on it. "I'll get some overheads."

He threw the phone into the air and watched as it did nothing to counter the effects of gravity, the phone hitting the ground and bouncing twice before disappearing over the lip of the grave.

Morgan rolled his eyes and shook his head. "I wish you'd stop doing that, Grave."

"Yes, sir," said Grave meekly. He quickly changed the subject. "The body was discovered by that reporter, Pippa Wobbly. Would you like me to interview her?"

Morgan looked around and spotted her standing next to Grave's father and Ida Notion. Wobbly appeared to be interviewing them. "Shit, get those two away from her. The mayor will have my ass if those two show up in the papers, or worse, on television."

"No problem."

"And no, I don't want you interviewing her. Leave that to Snoot. It's her case, and here she comes, anyway."

Grave looked down the hill. Detective Snoot was jogging up the hill on her twig-like legs in a way that suggested she never ran and perhaps had never mastered walking. "As you wish, sir, but this death may be linked more to the conference center murder than to Clink."

"Well, we don't know that yet, now do we? Let Polk do his work. If it's not a Clink killing, you can run with it. Otherwise, it's Snoot's."

"All right, I'll go break them up."

"What about your phone?"

Grave considered leaving it there in the grave. "I'll come back for it."

He ducked under the crime scene tape and walked over to confront the three of them.

"Okay, okay," he said, putting an arm between Wobbly and his father, and moving his father away from her. "Dad, I need you over here. You, too, Ida."

"But I'm not finished talking to them," said Wobbly.

"You are now. Wait there a second while I talk to these two."

He pulled his father and Ida further aside, under a nearby tree. "Listen, dad, you know how Morgan feels about this. You simply have to stay out of the way."

"Well, I *won't!*"

"Dad, you can do whatever investigating you wish, but not here, not now."

His father grumbled, and nodded. "Then we'll be on our way. We still have a *plan*, you know."

"Yes, follow your plan, but no, you can't leave yet."

His father knew instantly what that meant. "You don't mean?"

"Yes, you're witnesses. We'll want to know how and when you got here and what you saw."

"Well, let me tell you, then, and we'll be on our way."

Grave shook his head. "No, I can't do the interview. You're my father, dad. I'll get Blunt to talk to you."

Grave looked for Blunt and saw what appeared to be a man, albeit blurry, walking back up the hill. "Stay here, under the tree, and I'll get him."

"Whatever," said his father.

Grave strode toward Blunt, passing Wobbly on the way. "I'll be with you in a minute, Ms. Wobbly."

She started to say something but he was already past her and striding purposively toward what looked like a vapor.

"Blunt, over here," said Grave.

"Yes, sir."

"I need you to take statements from my father, his friend Ida Notion, and Ms. Wobbly over there."

"Okay, I'll let you know what I find out."

"Um, no, report to Snoot on this, and then let's get back to work on the Potz case."

"Yes, sir. Are you sticking around or should I meet you somewhere."

"I'll stick around a while, but until Morgan says otherwise, this is Snoot's case. He thinks Clink did it."

"All right, I'll find you when I'm done. I have a few things I'd like to talk to you about."

"Great. Well, then, better get to it."

Blunt floated over to Wobbly, who seemed startled when he began talking to her. She glanced over at Grave, a look of concern on her face, and something else, disappointment perhaps in not being able to talk to Grave directly.

Grave smiled at her and shrugged. She turned back and began speaking, in a voice so soft Grave could not make out the words.

He scanned the scene. His father and Ida Notion were still standing silently under the tree. Morgan and Snoot were standing next to the grave as Polk and his team lifted the body out and onto a stretcher. All along the hillside, simdroid Morgan Freemans were searching for a weapon, the blue beams of their scanners moving back and forth across the grass. Down the lane, where all the vehicles were parked, he could see the unmistakable presence of Claire Fairly, the TV reporter, already reporting the news in the bright lights of her cameraman. And above it all, whirring in formation, were twenty simdrones named Larry searching, recording, and cataloging all their sensors detected—the whole carnival of murder on full display.

Grave knew they'd find nothing. It was Clink, all right, and that man didn't make mistakes.

A movement up the path caught his attention. Victoria, the docent, was sitting down on her bench, the one where they'd met before.

Maybe she saw something, thought Grave. He began walking up the path, waving as he went. She caught sight of him and waved back, smiling.

"Hello again, Victoria."

"Hello, sir, happy to see you."

Grave sat down beside her. "Quite a day."

"Oh, in what way, sir?"

Grave pointed at the scene down the path. "This."

She seemed confused. "What?"

"Oh, maybe you weren't aware. I'm afraid there's been a murder."

She didn't seem alarmed in the least. "Oh, that."

"So you knew?"

"Yes, news travels fast here." She began to giggle. "Who are those men that all look alike down there? I've never seen the like."

"Oh, they're Morgan Freeman simdroids."

"Morgan who?"

Grave chuckled. "Of course, you're too young to know. He was an actor, a fine one, with an amazing voice. If you like I can call one here to talk with us, and you'll see what I mean about the voice."

She shook her head. "No, that's okay."

Grave steered the conversation back to the murder. "Did you see anything, perhaps?"

"Of what?"

"The murder itself."

"Oh, no, I just heard about it."

"Did you know the victim, Mr. Sparks?"

"Not until quite recently. He's a strange one. Claims to see the future, you know."

"Yes, I talked with him earlier. By any chance did he mention his own death? I mean, if he could see the future, why not his own death."

"He did, actually, but seemed resigned to it."

"Did he tell you anything about the murderer?"

Victoria cocked her head, thinking. "A little. He mentioned someone in a hood, with a large knife."

"Did he mention a name?"

"Yes, a Mr. Bowie."

"Oh," said Grave, "that would be the name of the knife."

"Really?"

"Yes. Did he mention a Mr. Clink, Chester Clink?"

Victoria brightened, eyes wide. "Yes, yes he did. I'd completely forgotten until you said his name."

Grave stood up. "Please, come with me. The captain will want to hear your story."

Victoria didn't move. "I'd rather not."

"Come on, it's only a short way."

She balked, shaking her head vigorously. "No, I'm supposed to be *here*. This is where I belong. And besides, I've told you everything I know."

Grave bent down and whispered to her. "I know you're reluctant to leave your assigned station, but I'm sure Mr. Winter would approve in this case."

She shook her head, crossed her arms, and turned her body away from him. "No."

"Please, it's only a short way."

"No, I *musn't*."

Grave could see she wasn't going to change her mind. "Okay, then, wait here. I'll bring the captain to you."

He turned away and walked back down the path to the open grave. Polk had already left with the body, leaving Captain Morgan standing with Detective Snoot by the grave, watching the patrolmen and the drones scan the cemetery for the weapon. When Morgan saw Grave, he reached out and handed him his phone, which was dirty and dented.

Grave quickly pocketed the phone. "Sir, you can call off the search. It's definitely Clink."

"And what makes you so certain all of a sudden?"

"I just talked to one of his colleagues, who said Sparks had seen his own death and had specifically mentioned Clink and his Bowie knife."

Morgan brightened. "Wonderful. Let's bring him in and get a statement."

"He's a *her*, actually, a young docent here at the cemetery. She's right up the path."

Grave turned to point back toward the bench, then stopped in mid-point. She was gone. "Crap! She was right there."

"Don't worry," said Morgan, "we'll find her. She can't have gone far." He turned to Snoot. "Handle it. Call off the weapons search and find the girl."

"Yes, sir," said Snoot, immediately striding away, her hand whirling in the air, trying to get the attention of a simdrone.

"And bring her to the station," Morgan yelled after her.

He turned to Grave. "Now, as for you, your work is done here. Get back on the Potz case. And please, *please*, have a talk with your father. I've reached my limit."

"Yes, sir, I'll talk to him tonight. What about Blunt?"

"I've sent him on his way, too, along with that woman and your father."

"All right, sir, I'll be on my way. Good luck with this one."

Grave began walking down the path, headed for his Sprite. His father and Ida Notion were standing in the lights below, being interviewed by Claire Fairly.

"Oh, shit." He began to run.

23

After the effort of pulling his father and Ida Notion away from the persistent questioning of Claire Fairly, the cacophonous solace provided by the Sprite's gospel choir was a welcome relief. Some people required silence to think, but Grave was just the opposite. Give him loud gospel music, and he was in his zone, thinking away and sorting data, not that all his thoughts necessarily led in logical directions. He had a strange relationship with logic, which he felt was too restrictive to be relied on entirely. Where other detectives religiously followed the old Sherlock Holmes dictum—*once you eliminate the impossible, whatever remains, no matter how improbable, must be the truth*—Grave preferred his own, somewhat askew view of the world: *once you eliminate the truth, whatever remains, no matter how improbable, must be the impossible.* Critics of his approach pointed out that Grave, despite his efforts, had never solved a single crime, but had only been there at the end, when the crime was revealed in detail and logic could finally arrange all the elements.

So for Grave, trying to sort out two cases at once, with or without logic, was a challenge. Fortunately, the music stopped, replaced by the booming voice of the Reverend Bendigo Bottoms, offering up yet another commandment: THOU SHALT CELEBRATE GOD, NOT THYSELF.

"Brothers, sisters, I know you have done many good things in your life. Many, many good and worthy things. And yet, do not commit the sin of pride. Recognize that all you have achieved has come through God, who watches over us all.

"I know you are wondering why I'm offering up an extra commandment today. And I'll tell you why. Last night, I was invited to give a eulogy and final holy words for a dearly departed man of some accomplishment. You would recognize his name, I'm sure. But when I arrived at the gravesite, I was horrified—*horrified*—to see not a somber scene of mourning and reflection, but a spectacle, a sinful display of pride.

"Instead of the usual headstone festooned with flowers, I saw a tall obelisk topped by an array of monitors extolling in video the accomplishments and life of this man, whom I once respected, but now must cast down for pride and idolatry and disrespect for hallowed ground.

"We all die, brothers and sisters, but just as in life, we have choices to make in death. Heed this warning and keep clear of the Crab Cove Cinema Cemetery. It is an abomination."

Grave detected a heavy sigh at the end of the reverend's soliloquy, and then the gospel music blared out once more, returning him to his thoughts, which had now been refocused by the reverend. He had to solve the Potz case and forget about Chester Clink.

Even that thought flew out of his head entirely when he turned the corner to his house and saw Charlize on the lawn, going through her Karate routine with four opponents, holograms all, and programmed to the level of Black Belt, Ninth Degree. They were simply no match for her.

Grave was certainly no match for her, either. He was a devotee of Hap Wadoo, a form of self-defense program that focused on the four pillars of self-preservation—Deny, Delay, Deflect, and Depart—all skills promoting flight over fight. As such, the one thing Hap Wadoo wasn't was a martial art. Indeed, it was the latest trendy new thing, one of a burgeoning field of alternative programs known as the *partial arts*, which featured colorful achievement belts that could be earned without the burden of effort, discipline, or dedication. Over the past two years he had worked himself up from white belt, to puce, to chartreuse, mostly through attendance, and could now deny, delay, deflect, and depart with some modicum of skill.

Charlize stopped her routine abruptly, as she always did when the gospel choir turned the corner. She ran over to the car as he pulled into the driveway. "Simon, where have you been?"

Simon leaned his head out of the car. "Sorry, delayed a bit at the cemetery. Come on, get in. We need to talk to two men named Jimmy."

Charlize balked. "In this? No, give me five minutes, and I'll slip into something more appropriate—more sleuthy."

"*Sleuthy?* Is that even a word?"

"No, but my programming allows deviations from the norm to lighten the mood."

"And you think the mood needs to be lightened?"

"Oh, Simon, if you had seen your face when you arrived, you wouldn't be asking that question."

Simon sighed. "Okay, but make it quick."

She returned ten minutes later, her white karategi replaced by a form-fitting black pantsuit, cinched tightly at the waist by a golden belt. She had pulled her hair back into a ponytail, and for a proper "deviation," she wore a deerstalker hat. All she lacked to complete her Sherlock Holmes homage was an Inverness cape and a briar pipe, and perhaps a violin.

She slipped into the Sprite and waggled her eyebrows at him. "On, Watson. The game is afoot!"

24

Barry and June sat in front of the video control panel at Ramrod Robotics, reviewing the memory bank videos of the six simdroids at Pick 'n Pack. The only thing they had learned so far was how to pick crab meat, a lot of crab meat.

June sighed. "Well, this is tedious."

Barry chuckled. "I know, but nine-tenths of detective work is tedious."

"Dreary, even."

"Yes."

"Mind numbing."

Barry held up a hand. "Enough, I think you've made your point."

He scrolled the video forward, looking for places in the video where the simdroids had looked away from the crabs they were deconstructing with astonishing speed and precision.

"Wait, here we go." He stopped the tape, backed it up a bit, then pressed play.

The simdroid was looking up and across the picking table, where a man, definitely Mr. Potz, was shouting at another man, who had grabbed him by the collar and was pushing him backward, away from the table. A third man suddenly appeared, who was also shouting at Potz. Then a fourth man, clearly the manager, Lester Finn, was leaping into the fray, pulling the two apart, and shouting at them both to back off. Both men were red-faced and continued to shout at one another until the simdroid looked down again and resumed picking.

"Crap," said Barry. "If we only had sound."

"Yes, but we at least have suspects and a possible motive. Who are those other men?"

Barry fumbled with a case folder he had brought along, which contained copies of Pick 'n Pack documents, including employee ID photos.

"Move it back a bit and freeze it," he said. "Yes, there."

Barry held up photo after photo, looking for a match. "Here, the one grabbing Potz is Jimmy Dibbs." He handed the photo to June.

"Yes, I agree."

He held up another photo and handed it to June. "And this is Jimmy Notch."

"Gotcha," said June.

"Well, maybe. Could be nothing."

"Or it could be something, a big something."

Barry put the photographs back in the folder. "Can we print out a few frames to show Morgan and Grave?"

"Yes, but didn't you say Grave was on his way to question them both?"

Blunt pulled out his phone. "Yes, you're right. Let me give him a buzz, and let him know what we've found."

"Reception sucks in here," said June. "You'd best go outside. I'll do the printing and meet you there."

"Right." Barry left the room and walked down the long stainless-steel corridor to the lobby, where he nodded to the receptionist, who couldn't see him at all.

Grave's phone rang and rang, then clicked over to voicemail.

He must be in that damned car of his, Barry thought.

He left a message at the tone, which involved four words ratcheted up to full urgency: "It's Blunt. Call me!"

25

Grave and Charlize drove in gospel-enforced silence to a trailer park on the south part of town, an area that used to be described as the other side of the tracks, but since the tracks had been removed long ago, the place was now commonly referred to as Hell's Crab Claw.

Not that it was anything like hell. The advent of robots and simdroids had performed miracles for the thirty or so small trailers that made up the park. Once dilapidated and overgrown by weeds, with more than a few junked cars on blocks, the park was now an actual park, with robot-trimmed lawns and shrubs, and well-maintained trailers, all color-coordinated to create the impression that you were walking into a modernist sculpture garden, not the abodes of low-income workers and their families.

Grave pulled up to an orange trailer trimmed in red and turned off the ignition. "Seventy-three, right?"

"Yes," said Charlize, "this is the place."

"Dibbs or Notch?"

"Dibbs."

"Okay, let's go."

They got out of the car and moved toward the trailer door, being careful to avoid a robotic lawnmower hard at work on the trailer's small patch of grass.

Grave was about to knock when his phone rang. It was Blunt.

"Well, it's about time," said Blunt. "Listen, we may have

something."

Grave listened, offering up *uh-huhs* as appropriate, and then clicked off.

"What was that?" said Charlize.

"A development. Seems a fight broke out between Mr. Potz and both Dibbs and Notch."

"The simdroid videos?"

"Yes. Anyway, we'll see if Dibbs here will admit to it."

"Right."

Grave approached the steps, but knocked on the door without climbing them. He could hear the muted sounds of shuffling feet, and then the door swung open, revealing a tall, muscular man in jeans and a tee shirt filling the doorway and staring down at them. With him came the smell of beer and pizza and something else, something rotten. In an instant, the man worked his face from a frown to a sneer to a snarl, his dark eyes fixed on them like a shark.

"What do *you* want?" he, um, snarled, lending credence to Grave's interpretation of the man's expression.

Grave held up his badge.

"I ain't done *nothin'*." His eyes darted back and forth between Grave and Charlize as if looking for the right person to blame, finally settling on Grave.

Grave attempted a calming smile. "Of course not, Mr. Dibbs. We're just here to ask a few questions about the late Mr. Potz."

"Oh, that. I just heard about it on TV. Terrible thing, but then again, he was going to die anyway."

"Indeed," said Grave, looking past Dibbs to the darkened interior of the trailer. "May we come in?"

Dibbs stepped back and waved them in. "Sure, why not."

Grave and Charlize stepped into the trailer, which was the antithesis of the trailer's exterior. The place was a wreck. A sink full of dishes, a table scattered with uneaten pizza crusts, and pizza boxes and empty beer cans littering the floor.

Dibbs caught their expressions and threw up his hands. "I try to keep it tidy, but it gets away from me at times. Here, let me clear off the table."

He swept his arm across the table and its bench seats, beer cans and pizza crusts flying to the floor, then motioned Grave and Charlize to sit down opposite him. Grave sat down.

"I shall stand," said Charlize. She knew that Grave would do the questioning, and she also knew her role was to protect Grave in the event that Dibbs got violent. She began pacing back and forth, surveying the room.

"Suit yourself," said Dibbs, sitting down and looking at Grave. His face was red from drinking, and as they talked, he scratched at his grizzled days-old beard. "Is she a droid?"

Grave nodded. "Yes."

"What's with the hat?"

"Um, she just likes hats."

Dibbs looked at Charlize Holmes, who had found a trash bag and was busy cleaning, and then turned back to Grave. "Lucky you. I had one just like her last week, down at the Red Crab Zone. They're beasts in bed, but I guess you already know that."

"Yes," said Grave, trying to shake off the image. "Now, to the point, do you know of anyone who would want to do Mr. Potz harm?"

Dibbs was shaking his head even before Grave finished asking the question. "No, the man was a saint. Everyone loved him."

"What about you? I understand he was the one who fired you."

"Nah, he was just acting for Mr. Finn. I don't blame Potz. Finn's the asshole behind it, replacing me and the others with those damned simdroids." He glanced over at Charlize. "No offense."

"None taken," said Charlize, taking a step to her left, giving her greater leverage if the need arose.

"Tell me about that," said Grave, "the firing, how it went down."

Dibbs raised his eyes to the ceiling, as if trying to recall the events. "We had just finished our lunch break, and when we came back to the picking area, there were them damned simdroids in our places, picking away, doing *our* jobs."

"And then Mr. Potz told you you were fired?"

"Yes, with Mr. Finn standing behind him, looking all too pleased with himself."

"And how did you all react?"

"Well, we exchanged some angry looks, but took it like men. Grabbed our gear from our lockers, and left."

"So there was no violence, no threats?"

Dibbs looked down at the table, then shook his head. "No, nothing like that."

"And you didn't hold a grudge against Potts, want to get back at him?"

Dibbs' eyes went wide. "Here, what are you saying? I'd never lift a finger to harm that poor man. But Finn, him I'd like to meet in a dark alley sometime."

"What about Jimmy Notch? How did he react to the firing?"

Dibbs seemed startled by the question, nervous. "He was behind me when they did it. Couldn't see his face, but he done nothin', just like me. Anyways, you best ask him. He's just three trailers down the line, the blue one with the purple door."

"We'll do that. What about the other workers let go?"

Dibbs shrugged. "They never said a word, at least not to me. Banged their lockers a bit when we were leaving, but again, I think they were just angry at Finn and the whole simdroid thing."

"And what are you doing now?"

Dibbs looked puzzled.

"I mean, for a job."

"Oh, nothing yet. Livin' on the SDA. Gettin' by."

Grave was well aware of the SDA, the Simdroid Displacement Allowance, which provided a living wage to anyone displaced by a simdroid or robot. It was the coming thing, as more and more workers found themselves without a job, with little hope of finding future work in this new world of robocapitalism.

"Right," said Grave, "right." He pushed himself up from the table. "That's all for now, but we may have additional questions later."

"Whatever."

Grave and Charlize left the trailer, the door clicking shut behind them.

"He's lying," said Charlize.

"I know."

"Then why not bring him in?"

"Oh, we probably will, but I want to talk to Jimmy Notch first, and maybe Mr. Finn. He's been lying, too."

"Right." She pulled a small plastic bag from her pocket.

"What's that?"

"A beer can, a napkin, and some pubic hairs."

"Pubic hairs?"

"From the toilet. To see if we have a match with the prints and DNA from the van."

She really should be on the squad, thought Grave. "Good work. Now, let's see if we can rouse Jimmy Notch."

They began walking down the line of trailers, then stopped with a start. There was a hearse parked in front of a blue trailer with a purple door. A body was being loaded into the back of it, and the segmented insect that was Pippa Wobbly was standing there, watching, along with an elderly man Grave presumed was from the funeral home.

26

Grave and Charlize walked the final steps to the hearse, Grave nodding at Ms. Wobbly, then flashing his badge at the old man with a cane standing next to the hearse. He was short and frail and dressed all in black, except for gray gloves and a red scarf he had wrapped around his neck, an odd thing on such a warm day. His hair was perfectly white and combed over with great care to hide his bald pate.

"I'm Detective Simon Grave. What's happened?"

The man forced a smile, his beady, pale blue eyes giving Grave an appraising look. "One of my patients, I'm afraid."

"And you are?"

"Oh, of course, the name is Zorn. Doctor James Zorn."

Grave recognized the name immediately. "I see. I believe you're my father's doctor as well."

Zorn raised his bushy white eyebrows, then frowned. "Why, yes, Jacob Grave. I hear he's told you the grim news."

"Yes, and I'd like to talk to you about that at some point, but for now, what exactly has happened here?"

Wobbly spoke up, words spilling from her. "He was dead, in the bath, I found him. The front door was ajar, you see, so I knocked and came in. There was water everywhere."

"And that would be Mr. Notch?"

"Yes," said Wobbly. "I wanted to interview him about the Potz murder."

Grave frowned at her. "I see. So you discovered the body. Did you call the police?"

She shook her head. "I was about to, and then Doctor Zorn arrived."

"He had called me," said Zorn. "He was having difficulties, thought he was having a heart attack."

Grave was incredulous. "Wait, you make *house calls?*"

Zorn shrugged. "People are healthier and healthier these days. The number of patients I see is dwindling, so I have time. And besides, doctors are in competition for patients now, so any extra service helps."

"All right," said Grave. "So you arrive, with a *hearse?*"

"No, I called them after I arrived. He was in the bath, as she said, and quite dead."

"Drowned?"

Zorn seemed startled. "No, of course not. A heart attack, pure and simple."

"Yes," said Wobbly. "He was above water, sitting back." Her voice began to tremble. "It was awful."

"From the looks of things," said Zorn, "he wasn't able to reach his medicine."

"Or he dropped it," said Wobbly. "There were pills all over the place."

"All right," said Grave. "Let's have a look."

He motioned them toward the door of the trailer, but Zorn broke away. "I'll just be a second."

He raced as fast as an old man with a cane can race, which was slightly faster than slow, handed the driver an envelope, and then hurried back to the others with equal cane-clacking speed as the hearse slowly moved away.

Grave narrowed his eyes on him. "What was that envelope?"

"Death certificate."

"You bring death certificates *with* you?"

Zorn laughed nervously. "No, of course not. The funeral home brought them along."

"Which home was that?"

"Satin Passages, that new one out on She-Crab Avenue."

Grave turned to Charlize. "Give them a call, and tell them to hold the body for a possible autopsy. Then call Polk for a pickup."

"Yes, sir." She stepped away and began tapping on the keypad on her palm.

Grave turned back to Zorn, who was wringing his hands.

"Autopsy? Whatever for? I know a heart attack when I see one."

"Yes, I'm sure you do. No offense. Just getting a second opinion. Come on, show me this bathtub."

Wobbly led the way into the trailer, a double wide, more luxurious than the Dibbs trailer, and neat as a pin, save for the wet carpeting. The bathroom was toward the end, down a narrow hallway. Unlike the Dibbs trailer, the whole place smelled antiseptic clean.

The tub was empty and there was no sign of pills.

"You mentioned pills. Where are they?"

Zorn sighed heavily. "I flushed them."

"What? Why would you do that?"

"They're deadly to pets. His cat, you see."

Grave looked around. There had been no cat in the living room or hallway, and most particularly, the place didn't smell of cat. "And where is this so-called cat?"

"Outside, I guess," said Wobbly. "There was no cat when I got here, anyway."

"He *has* a cat, detective," said Zorn. "A Maine Coon Cat. I know because I've been here before."

"All right, all right," said Grave, turning to Zorn. "And what exactly was this medicine?"

"Thalazonimide Hydrochloride, for angina pectoris."

"Really? I thought there were cures for that. Replacement hearts and so forth."

"For most people, yes, but not for poor Mr. Notch."

"I see. By any chance do you have the prescription bottle?"

Zorn fumbled in his pocket, drew out an amber-colored vial, and offered it to Grave.

"No, just set it on the sink there if you don't mind."

Zorn complied. "Detective, are we done here?"

"Soon," said Grave. "Would you mind waiting outside for a minute?" He motioned them toward the door.

Zorn and Wobbly shrugged and left.

Grave called after them. "And give Charlize your contact information while you're at it."

Zorn called back. "The droid with the hat?"

"Yes, her."

He turned his attention back to the vial on the counter, taking out a small evidence bag and slipping the vial into it. Then he bent down and retrieved the true prize from under the sink. A small yellow pill, partially dissolved by the water on the floor. He plopped it into another bag and put both bags in his pocket. He scanned the bathroom one more time, then went outside.

Zorn and Wobbly were standing together, not talking, rocking from foot to foot impatiently. Charlize was off to the side, still on her hand phone.

"Did you give her your information?"

They both nodded.

"Okay, then, you're free to go."

Zorn moved like a horse out of the gate, walking and clacking his cane as quickly as he could manage to his car, an old Teslonic Hover XL, and accelerating away with a quiet whir. *He really must be having hard times*, thought Grave. *An old clunker like that, for a doctor?*

Wobbly lingered. "Detective, would it be possible to meet later, perhaps have a coffee?"

Grave could feel a blush coming on, and tried his best to suppress it, but seeing her now, out of her insect clothing and looking more than attractive was just too much. Her lavender eyes seemed to draw him in, embrace him, dance with him, hold him spellbound, leaving him dumbstruck, as if he had been touched by an angel.

Grave glanced nervously at his watch. "Yes, how about 2:30," he stammered. "At the Skunk 'n Donuts on Main?"

"Perfect," she said, turning to go.

He called after her. "If you get there first, order me a chocolate donut and a decaf, will you?"

She smiled back at him. "Of course."

He watched her walk to her car and drive away.

"Well, that's interesting," said Charlize, coming up behind him.

"What?"

"The way you looked at her. Do I detect romance in the offing?"

He smiled and started walking back to the Sprite. "You never know."

27

When Grave and Charlize arrived at the morgue, Polk was bent over the body of Eddie Sparks, his gloved fingers tracing the many knife wounds. Captain Morgan and Detective Snoot were watching him work, and nodded at Grave and Charlize when they walked in, although Morgan was clearly not happy about the presence of Charlize.

"Any conclusions?" said Grave.

Polk continued his work without looking up. "It's the work of Chester Clink, all right. Number of wounds, length, depth—it all fits."

"The only question is why him," said Captain Morgan. "Why a man, and why has he chosen to divert from his MO?"

"Perhaps Mr. Sparks was viewed as a threat," offered Charlize.

Morgan bristled. "Please stay out of this."

She nodded and took a step back.

"No," said Grave, "she's right, that could be the very reason."

Detective Snoot, who'd been eyeing them with displeasure since their arrival, spoke up. "Then he would have been a threat for the past twelve years. Why not kill him long ago? Why now?"

"The last time I looked," said Grave, "Sparks' whereabouts were unknown. Nobody knew where he was, or even *if* he was. The man just flat out disappeared."

Morgan gave him a puzzled look. "So what do you think, then?"

"I think Clink happened upon Sparks accidentally. Like me, he must have been at the cemetery for some reason. Only *he* recognized Sparks and I didn't."

Morgan turned to Snoot. "Head on back there and see if Clink talked to Mr. Winter."

"Yes, sir." She started to leave.

"And talk to Victoria again, the docent," said Grave. "She might have seen something."

Snoot shook her head. "We never found her, but if she's there this time, I'll chat her up."

"Sounds right," said Morgan. "Get to it."

Morgan watched her go, then turned to Grave. "So what about the Potz case?"

Grave brought them up to speed on his and Charlize's talk with Jimmy Dibbs and the death of Jimmy Notch, including the evidence they'd collected from both trailers.

"Okay," said Polk, "I'll see if we have a match with the prints and DNA from the van, and run some tests to determine what this pill is."

"Good," said Morgan. He turned to Grave. "I don't suppose you doubled back to Dibbs to get any information he may have had about Notch."

Grave grimaced. He should have done just that. "No, sorry, but I'll have Blunt do that. Which reminds me, where is Blunt?"

Everyone shrugged.

"I'll give him a call when I leave," said Grave.

"Hang on," said Morgan. "Sounds like we have a viable suspect in Dibbs. Let's not just talk to him; let's bring him in. Polk, how long before we can get a match?"

"I'll get right on it. Tomorrow morning perhaps."

"Good, we can detain Dibbs that long. Now, as to the Notch thing. Does it trouble anyone that that reporter, Ms. Wobbly, was at the scene of all three murders?"

"Quite the coincidence," said Polk.

"The universe is rarely so lazy," said Charlize.

Morgan looked bewildered. "What?"

"A quote, sir," said Charlize. "Sherlock Holmes."

Morgan was about to slap her down, but Grave interceded.

"But perhaps it is just that, a coincidence," he said. "At any rate, she asked to talk with me this afternoon, so I'll press her on that point. Apparently, she's working on a story about the Potz murder, so I'll see what she's dug up at least."

"All right, you do that. This whole Notch death smells funny to me," said Morgan. "I mean, who makes a house call?"

"The analysis will tell the tale," said Polk. "And the Notch autopsy." He glanced at his watch. "Where is that body? Should have been here by now."

Grave looked around the examination room. "Speaking of bodies, where's Potz?"

"I released his body to Satin Passages about an hour ago."

"So soon?"

"Not really. We have all the evidence we need."

"Captain," said Grave. "Perhaps we should have another talk with Doctor Zorn. Two suspicious deaths. A house call of all things. And a botched diagnosis on Potz."

"Sounds right," said Morgan. "You go ahead and meet with Ms. Wobbly. Blunt can pick up Dibbs, and I'll have Snoot swing by and get Doctor Zorn after she's finished at the cemetery."

"Right," said Grave, nodding to Charlize and heading for the door.

"We'll get 'em in," said Morgan, "and do our good cop, bad cop on the both of them."

28

Grave spent the drive to Skunk 'n Donuts thinking about the suspects. Dibbs seemed a likely candidate for the Potz murder. Shirley had said the driver was human and named Jimmy, and Jimmy Dibbs certainly had a motive and had clearly lied to him. If his prints and DNA matched those they found in the van, he would be the murderer. On the other hand, if there was no match, they'd be back to square one, with a number of questions. Could Jimmy Notch have done it? Why had the murderer moved the body to the beach instead of just leaving it in the van?

But with Jimmy Notch now dead, the likelihood that he had murdered Potz seemed unlikely. It must be Dibbs, but would that mean Dibbs had also killed Notch? Why would he have done that? And what about Doctor Zorn? Two of his patients were dead, and he'd misdiagnosed at least one of them. On the other hand, why on earth would he kill his own patients? And he was so old and frail, it all seemed so unlikely.

Then there was Lester Finn, the manager at the Pick 'n Pack. Why had he lied about what went down at the time of the firing? And what about Pippa Wobbly, who'd been first on the scene now for three murders, which stretched probability and coincidence to the limits. Did she have any ties to the victims?

And then there was Chester Clink. Was the murder of Eddie Sparks an isolated murder, or was it somehow linked to the others in ways Grave could not yet fathom?

Charlize's voice broke him from his querulous reverie. "Whoa, here we are, sir. Stop!"

Grave braked just in time to pull into the only vacant parking spot in front of the Skunk 'n Donuts. "Whew, thanks."

"What on earth were you thinking about?"

"The case, or cases. There's a lot to sort."

"I have a theory," said Charlize, holding her hand up to her mouth as if she were smoking a pipe.

Grave laughed. "Well, hold on to that. Let's see what Ms. Wobbly has to say. We can discuss your theory at home."

"As you wish," she said, dropping her invisible pipe to her lap.

Pippa Wobbly was easy to spot when they walked into the coffee shop. She was the only customer there. And it was also clear she had not ordered for him.

Grave waved at her, then ordered a chocolate donut and a cup of the new simcoffee that was rapidly replacing the dwindling supply of real coffee, the latest effect of global warming, which was killing off coffee plantations at a rapid clip. The new coffee, a blend of herbs and roots and the wonders of chemistry, was passable if not delicious, and came with the same energizing jolt as the real thing, or at least the fading memory of the real thing.

Grave collected his simcoffee and donut, paid the barista, and walked with Charlize to the booth at the back of the shop, where Pippa Wobbly waited, smiling up at them as they sat down. Grave had to admit he was strongly attracted to her, particularly her lavender eyes, which were like tractor beams. He just couldn't look away.

"Nice hat," she said to Charlize.

Charlize smiled back. "Thank you."

Wobbly turned to Grave. "And thank you for meeting with me."

"Not at all, I'm sure we have as many questions as you do about the murders."

Wobbly gave him a surprised look. "*What*, no, I just thought you'd like to know what I know—what I've found out so far."

"Of course," said Grave. "Well, then."

"Right," said Wobbly, pulling out a notebook and flipping it open. "There are a lot of people dying in Crab Cove, and I'm not talking about murders."

"She's right," said Charlize. "My own investigation revealed the same thing. More deaths by far than previous years."

"Absolutely, but there's more," said Wobbly. "The demographics are wildly skewed toward the elderly."

"Wouldn't that be a natural result of an aging population?" said Grave.

"That's what I thought at first, but no, a natural result would have followed a predictable curve, but what we're seeing is a dramatic spike, almost like an extinction event."

"I saw that, too," said Charlize. "And the manner of death has also changed dramatically. A shift away from accidental deaths—you know, the usual drownings and auto accidents we have here—to death by disease. Inoperable tumors, cancers, heart attacks."

"But when you take away accidents and drownings," said Grave, "isn't murder and death by disease all that's left? I mean, we're down to brain cancer and pancreatic cancer, right?"

"Yes," said Charlize, "but the incidence and prevalence of those cancers is off the charts."

"Exactly," said Wobbly. "But more to the point, when I mentioned this to Mr. Winter at C4 and Mr. Smith at the garden cemetery, they acted like I was crazy."

"Interesting," said Grave. "Winter said much the same thing to me. Said his increases were due to better marketing, that he was getting a bigger share of the market."

Wobbly nodded. "And I got the same reaction from the director at Satin Passages."

"On the other hand," said Charlize, "they are both new enterprises, so they may not have enough experience to judge the increase one way or the other."

"True," said Grave, "but Eddie Sparks said there was an absolute increase."

"Who?" said Wobbly.

"Sparks, the body in the grave."

"Oh, I didn't know that." She scribbled a note in her notebook. "Wait, wasn't he connected to the Clink murders?"

Her question startled him. "Yes, but how would you know that?"

"I've been following the Clink story for *years.*" She seemed defensive.

"Really? I thought you were new to town."

Wobbly laughed nervously. "I am, but *everyone* knows about Clink."

Grave had to admit that the case was an international sensation, and an embarrassment to Crab Cove. "Right. Anyway, where does that leave us with this increase in deaths?"

"As dramatic as the rise has been," said Charlize. "It could be natural."

Wobbly leaned across the table. "How so?"

"Well, it's interesting. I did a search for any studies related to deaths in Crab Cove and came up with a study done by the Crab Cove Institute for Crab Research, which postulated that changes in crab meat may be responsible for an increase in cancer deaths."

"Wow," said Grave. "Why haven't we heard of that before?"

"Well, it's your human nature again," said Charlize. "Resistance to change, profit motive, call it what you will. The fact is, the Chamber of Commerce and the mayor quashed the whole thing, even persuaded the institute to dismiss the researcher."

"Then again," said Grave, "it was just one study."

"Well, *here*, yes, but there are other studies. San Francisco, New Orleans, even Norway, and all indicating an increase in cancer deaths from the consumption of crab meat."

"Global warming again?" said Wobbly.

"It's unclear," said Charlize, "but that seems to be the trend for just about everything, right?"

"All right," said Grave. "So we may be dealing more with an environmental factor than anything suspicious."

"Maybe," said Wobbly.

"At any rate," said Grave, "I have a few questions for you."

Wobbly raised her eyebrows, a bit surprised. "Well, okay, *what?*"

"I can't help wondering why you were the first person to arrive on the scene of three consecutive murders."

Wobbly shrugged. "Just coincidence."

Grave stared at her, but she didn't so much as blink. "Perhaps," he said finally. "Let's start with the Potz murder."

"I was there, as you well know, to cover the conference for my paper. And you saw me at the reception, eating like a little pig. I thought a walk would do me good, and bingo, there's poor Mr. Potz."

"And Mr. Sparks?"

"I had just interviewed Mr. Winter, and when I came out, I saw a murder of crows hovering around that grave. I decided to have a look, and so that's that one."

"And Mr. Notch."

"I had just talked to Mr. Finn at the Pick 'n Pack, and learned about the firings. Thought there might be a connection to the Potz murder, so I went to see Notch."

"Had you talked to Mr. Dibbs as well?"

"He's next on my list."

"Right. So tell me about Notch."

"I've already told you. I arrived. The door was ajar, so I went in and discovered the body. And then about a minute later Doctor Zorn arrived."

"Tell me about that. Did he seem alarmed?"

"In what way?"

"You know, he was coming to see a patient who thought he was having a heart attack."

"Oh, I see what you mean. Yes, he rushed in, seemed very concerned."

"And when exactly did he take care of the pills?"

"Almost immediately. Asked me to look around for the cat. He was very concerned about it."

"So you left him alone in the bathroom?"

"Um, yes, but just for a few minutes. In any event, I couldn't find the cat. I assume it ran outside."

"Wait," said Charlize. "You said the door was ajar when you arrived."

"That's right."

Charlize turned to Grave. "Don't you see?"

Grave didn't. "See what?"

Charlize gave an exasperated groan. "The cat could certainly have opened a door left ajar, but would it be able to close the door behind it?"

"So the cat was already gone when I got there," said Wobbly.

"Maybe. Did you leave the door open when you came in?"

"No, I shut it behind me."

"So, yes," said Charlize, "it was probably already outside."

"Why would you shut the door?" said Grave.

"I don't know. I guess I'm a bit anal about such things."

Grave smiled and shook his head. "So where does that leave us?"

"With a few possibilities," said Charlize. "The cat could have run by Ms. Wobbly without her seeing it."

"I doubt that," said Wobbly. "I'm pretty observant."

"Or," continued Charlize, "Notch left the door ajar so the cat could come in or go out."

Wobbly frowned. "I wouldn't do that, would you? Take a bath with the front door open? No way."

"But it's possible," said Grave.

"Yes," said Charlize, "but there's more. Perhaps we're dealing with foul play, and the killer left the door ajar in his rush to leave the trailer."

"Or to minimize noise," said Wobbly. "That door is tight. I really had to slam it shut."

"Which would have alerted anyone nearby," said Grave.

Charlize giggled, but not in a way that would suggest she had just heard or thought of something funny. Rather, it was a giggle prompted by the result of the logical processing of available information and data. "Ah, the curious incident of the dog in the night-time," she said, holding up an invisible pipe to her lips.

Grave and Wobbly gave her puzzled looks.

"What?" said Grave.

"A Sherlock Holmes quote, sir. And what was curious was that there was no dog at all."

"So you think—"

"Maybe there was no *cat* at all. Maybe Doctor Zorn made it up to get Ms. Wobbly to leave the room."

"And to give him a reason to flush the pills," said Grave, beaming at Charlize. "Excellent!"

Wobbly was shaking her head. "But he was so *insistent* about the cat."

"It doesn't matter," said Charlize. "Cat or no cat, he could have made up the story about the pills being poisonous to cats."

"Yes, I guess," said Wobbly.

Grave suddenly remembered his first impression of entering the trailer. "Wait, wait, cat or no cat may indeed be the question. The trailer didn't smell like cat when I walked in."

"Yes, you're right," said Wobbly. "So there wasn't a cat after all."

Charlize was shaking her head. "Or there was a cat, but maybe it wasn't a *real* cat."

In the history of dropping jaws, none but Grave's had dropped so quickly and so dramatically. "Oh," he said, "oh."

Wobbly was completely confused. "What?"

Charlize smiled. "It seems very possible that our Mr. Dibbs may have owned a *simcat.*"

"Oh," said Wobbly.

"And perhaps most important," said Grave, "the simcat could have witnessed *everything.*"

Wobbly looked puzzled.

"Video," said Charlize.

Wobbly's eyebrows assumed the full-upright position. "Wow, I guess we'd better find that cat."

Grave nodded. "Yes, and one more thing. Notch's cellphone."

Wobbly was startled. "What?"

"Yeah, it just hit me," said Grave. "If he made a call from his tub, where is his cellphone?"

29

Sergeant Blunt parked his squad car in front of the trailer, close to its front door, so he could block Dibbs' escape if the man made a run for it. He was being overly cautious—most people couldn't see him, so he always had the element of surprise in his favor—but he didn't want to blow the collar. With a baby on the way, a hoped-for promotion to lieutenant would be more than a good thing, so the importance of everything he did now seemed magnified.

He got out of the car and walked to the front door, which he could see was slightly ajar. He knocked. "Mr. Dibbs, police."

Silence.

He pulled out his pistol and carefully pushed open the door. "Police. I'm coming in."

A cat jumped out at him and quickly raced away, leaving Blunt gasping for breath. He had almost shot the thing, or more accurately, himself.

He calmed himself and walked in. The place reeked of pizza and beer, and something else, a hint of disinfectant, but sweet, almost fruity. Blunt took a deep breath. *Chloroform.*

He moved from room to room, switching on lights as he went.

No Dibbs.

The drawers to the man's chest of drawers were all open and empty, and there was no suitcase to be seen. *He's long gone,* thought Blunt. *Or someone's taken him.*

He holstered his pistol and went back to the small kitchen, where he opened cabinet after cabinet until he found what he was looking for—a large bottle of chloroform and a stack of large gauze pads big enough to cover a person's mouth and nose. He didn't have any gloves with him, so he decided not to touch the bottle, although from the smell, its cap seemed to be loose. Whoever used it last must have been in a hurry. He closed the cabinet door, leaving the bottle for the forensics team, then went outside and pulled out his cellphone. Captain Morgan picked up on the third ring.

"Morgan here, what's up?"

"Sir, it looks like Dibbs has made a run for it."

"Damn!"

"But he's our man, sir. I found chloroform in his kitchen cabinet."

"So *he's* Jimmy the driver."

"Looks like."

"Okay, I'll put out an APB on him. See if the neighbors saw anything, and then get back here."

"Yes, sir." Blunt clicked off and then scanned the lane. Not a single person walking around, just that damned cat, scratching at the door of a trailer a short ways down the lane.

He would have to go trailer to trailer. He pulled out his cellphone again and began walking to the closest trailer.

"Hon, it's me. Looks like I'll be a little late tonight."

June wasn't happy. "Barry, I thought you'd assemble the crib tonight. You've been putting it off for weeks."

Blunt rolled his eyes. "I'll do it, I'll do it, however late I come home."

"Wonderful. You're such a dear."

He could almost see her smiling. "Right, then. I'd better get back to work. See you tonight."

He clicked off and put away his cellphone, which almost immediately began ringing again. *What did June want now?*

He tugged out the phone and looked at the display. It wasn't June at all.

"Yes, sir," said Blunt.

The voice of Detective Grave filled his ear. "Blunt, are you at the trailer park?"

"Yes. Dibbs has taken a runner, it seems. I'm going house to house to see if anyone saw him leave."

"Wow, really? That's good, very good, but listen. Have you seen a cat?"

Blunt had expected more praise from his apparent solving of the case, not a strange request about a cat. "A cat? Yes, almost shot one, in fact. He ran right out of Dibbs' trailer when I arrived. Almost scared me to death. Why do you ask?"

"Because we need to find that cat."

"But the captain said —"

"Blunt, you can do the door to door later. We need that cat. It's a simcat, and it may have seen *everything*."

Blunt looked quickly down the lane to where he had seen the cat before. No cat.

"I'll do my best, sir."

"Did you bring along any simdrones? They could help."

"No, not a single Larry, sir."

"All right, start looking and I'll send some along."

"Okay, will do."

Grave wasn't finished. "And Blunt, when you find it, bring it back to the station. I have to take Charlize home, but I'll be at the station in less than an hour."

"Right."

"And bring June. We need to know *everything* about simcats."

"Um, very well."

The phone went silent; Grave had clicked off. Blunt started to call June, but then stopped. No need to disappoint her about the evening until he had found the damned cat.

He began looking, the whir of approaching simdrones growing whirier.

30

Charlize had been pouting the whole way home, angry that Grave was not taking her to the station to help with the interrogation, but as soon as they turned into the driveway, she squealed with delight and leaped out of the Sprite, which had barely come to a halt, the gospel choir still ratcheted up to ungodly decibels.

A large wooden crate was sitting at the top of the driveway, and judging from its size, it could be only one thing: the new electric motor. Charlize was dancing around it like it was a diamond.

"Simon, Simon, come see!"

Grave got out of the car and walked over to the crate, which was labeled with various cautions and instructions that made Grave feel uneasy. Just opening the crate might be dangerous.

He rapped his knuckles on the top of it. "The new engine?"

Charlize giggled. "The *motor*, yes, wait till you see it."

Before he could speak, she was racing for the front door, no doubt to get a crowbar from her workshop in the basement.

He looked at the crate again. The *this-side-up* arrow was pointing down. *Well, that's not good.*

Charlize came bounding down the steps with a crowbar. "Step back and let me at it."

"Wait," said Grave, pointing at the arrow.

Charlize frowned, set down the crowbar, and then lifted the crate, turning it right side up and setting it back down. Grave knew she was strong, but not *this* strong.

"Jeez," he said, "that must be five hundred pounds."

Charlize smiled at him. "Close. It's actually six hundred seventy-seven pounds, four ounces, give or take."

Grave shook his head in awe. "Well, open it up. Let's see this marvel."

Seconds later, the lid and the four sides to the crate were lying on the driveway, revealing a bright red motor with wires going this way and that. Charlize was stroking it like it was a new pet cat.

"Isn't it beautiful?"

"Yes, but it's *huge.* Will it fit?"

Charlize laughed. "Of course it will fit."

She walked over to the Sprite and opened its hood. "I just need to pull the old engine, and drop in the new one. Should have it ready for you by tomorrow morning."

"No, I have to drive to the station *now.*"

Charlize was shaking her head. "No, you don't. I've called a cab for you."

Grave hated the new driverless cabs that had taken over Crab Cove. "I'd rather not."

Charlize said nothing, but pointed down the street, where a vehicle was turning the corner.

Grave groaned when he saw it. "Not a *hover*cab."

"Yes, what's wrong?"

"They make me feel queasy. There's no road feel."

Charlize put her hands on her hips and cocked her head. "Well, it's here and you're going. I have to get to work."

With that, she turned and raced back into the house to get her tools.

Grave walked to the hovercab and climbed in. "To the police station, please. But not too fast."

"As you wish," said a woman's voice coming from the dashboard. "For your safety, please fasten your seatbelt. Our trip today will take approximately four minutes. Sit back, relax, and listen to the latest neodisco tune by Quake, now sitting atop the charts for the thirty-first consecutive week, and brought to you today by the Crab Cove Cinema Cemetery, your gateway to the afterlife."

Grave groaned, buckled himself in, and grabbed onto the seat, his knuckles going white as the hovercab sped away to the throb and thrum of neodisco. Clearly, his wish was not her command.

31

Detective Amanda Snoot tried to stay cool under the constant harangue coming from the back seat. Doctor Zorn had not come quietly, so she had had to cuff him and load him into the squad car as his elderly receptionist had stood by screaming at her for "the injustice of it all."

She had arrived at the doctor's office just minutes before, after a fruitless trip to the cinema cemetery to question the docent Grave had mentioned. She had launched half a dozen simdrones, but not a single Larry had found anyone fitting the girl's description. Worse, Mr. Winter had checked the staff records, and there was not a single Victoria. Or so he said. She didn't much trust anything that came out of his mouth. He was a slippery one.

"I must *insist*," said Doctor Zorn from the back seat. "I must *insist* that you let me go. I have patients to see."

"Sir, as I have already explained to you, your presence is required down at the station."

"Well, I don't see why. I've already told you people all I know."

"We have questions."

Doctor Zorn let out an exasperated sigh that puffed its way to the back of Snoot's neck, making her cringe.

"What kind of questions?"

"You'll find out when we get there. Now just settle down, and we'll have you back in your office in no time. If you cooperate, that is."

"*Cooperate?* I've *been* cooperating. So this is the thanks I get for being a good citizen."

Detective Snoot rolled her eyes, put the car in gear, and accelerated away, wondering if it would be appropriate to hit the lights and siren, and run all the lights at high speed to get to the station faster.

"This is *ridiculous*," shouted Zorn.

She hit the lights and siren.

32

Grave and Captain Morgan stood behind the two-way mirror and watched as Detective Snoot hustled a reluctant Doctor Zorn into the interrogation room, sat him down at the small table inside, and removed his cuffs. She took a quick glance at the mirror, rolled her eyes, and left Zorn to himself.

Morgan turned to Grave. "Are you sure you want to go through with this? I mean, it's pretty clear that Dibbs is our man. And you still look a little green from the hover ride."

Grave tried not to think of the ride to the station. "He may be our man, but there's something about Zorn and the death of Mr. Notch that smells of dead crab."

Morgan shrugged. "Well, all right. Go on in."

"Right. Let me know when Blunt arrives."

"The simcat thing?"

"Yes, it will be interesting to match what the simcat saw against what Doctor Zorn says happened."

"Okay, no problem."

Grave left the viewing room and headed for the door to the interrogation room. Snoot was waiting for him.

"Good luck with that one," she said.

Grave was surprised that she shared the same opinion of Zorn. Maybe they could work together after all. "Thanks, how did it go?"

"You'll see. He thinks he's being punished for being a good

citizen. The man is *insufferable.*"

Grave had to chuckle. "Yes, I know." He looked around the squad room. "Did you find Victoria?"

"No, and Winter says there's no such person employed there. Simdrones found nothing, but I don't trust the man. I think he's lying. He seemed very nervous."

"Right, I had the same feeling about him. Okay, I'll follow up after I talk to Doctor Zorn."

Snoot seemed relieved. "Great, and will you do me a big favor?"

Grave knew exactly what that favor was. "My father?"

"Yes, he's driving me *crazy.*"

"I'll talk to him."

"Good."

"So, anything on Clink from Mr. Winter?"

"No, I showed him a pic and he claimed never to have seen him. But again, I don't trust him."

"I know what you mean."

She glanced at her watch. "Anyway, the doctor is all yours." She gave him a devious smile and walked away.

Grave took a deep breath and walked into the room, sitting down opposite Doctor Zorn, who was fuming.

"This is *outrageous*," he shouted.

Grave smirked. "Not really, Doctor Zorn. We just have a few additional questions. You know, tying up loose ends."

Zorn pounded his fists on the table. "What loose ends? I responded to my patient's emergency call and found him dead of a heart attack. End of story."

Grave ignored the table-pounding and smiled at him. "Of course, that's probably *exactly* what happened."

"Then why am I here?" Zorn huffed.

"Loose—"

"*Ends*, yes I know that." He slumped back in his chair and crossed his arms. "So let's get on with it. What is so *loose* about these ends of yours?"

Grave stood up and began pacing, his eyes fixed on Zorn. "All ends have a beginning, so let's start there. You received a call from Mr. Notch. Tell me about that."

Zorn rolled his eyes. "All right, all right. He called me, and I could tell by the urgency in his voice that something was seriously wrong."

"What did he say, exactly?"

Zorn looked at the ceiling, trying to remember the exact words. "He said something like, 'Doc, come quick. I think it's my heart.'"

"And what did you say?"

"I told him to take two of his pills, and that I would be there immediately."

"But you didn't call an ambulance?"

Zorn looked chagrined. "No, I guess I should have, but the pills should have worked. They always had in the past."

"So this had happened before?"

"Yes, several times, in fact."

"I see, so you didn't see it as a real emergency."

"Exactly. Mr. Notch tended toward the dramatic. I thought it might have been another false alarm."

Grave sat back down. "Okay, so you arrive on the scene. What next?"

Zorn shrugged. "I went inside and found this woman, the reporter, what's her name, standing over Mr. Notch."

"Ms. Wobbly. Okay, back up. When you arrived, was the door to the trailer open, ajar, or shut?"

"I don't know, what difference does it make?"

"Answer, please."

Zorn slumped back in his chair, thinking. "It was shut."

"And did you knock?"

"No, of course not. The man had called me from his tub."

"He told you he was in the tub?"

"Yes, and he was afraid to move."

"So you just went right in."

"Yes, of course."

"And when you opened the door, did you perhaps see a cat?"

Zorn was about to answer, but there was a knock at the door.

Morgan stuck his head in and winked at Grave. "A moment, if you don't mind."

"Yes, sir." He stood up, placing both hands on the table, and hovered over Zorn. "I'll be right back, and we'll chat about the cat."

Zorn seemed mystified.

33

Grave left the interrogation room and followed Captain Morgan to his office, where he could see the clouds of Blunt and June pacing about.

"Good to see you, June," said Grave, trying to make her out. "Sort of."

A chuckle came from the cloud. "And you," she said.

"You're looking wonderful. When's the baby due?"

"Any day now. Can't wait."

Captain Morgan huffed. "I hate to break up the baby shower, but can we get on with it? What's all this about a cat?"

"Right," said Grave. "We have reason to believe that Notch's cat is a simcat and may have recorded everything."

"So where is this simcat?"

Blunt jumped in. "A good question, sir. I saw the cat when I first arrived at the trailer park. It was coming out of Dibbs' trailer, but I didn't think anything of it until Detective Grave called me. And by then, it had disappeared."

Grave was shaking his head. "So, I take it you didn't find the cat."

"No, sir. We searched—me and the Larrys—but no cat, real or otherwise."

Captain Morgan was not known for his attention to details, but for some reason, a significant detail clicked into place.

"Excuse me, but what makes you think the cat belonged to Notch?"

Grave wasn't following. "What?"

"The cat ran out of *Dibbs'* trailer, right? So who's to say it wasn't *his* cat."

Blunt had already put two and two together, at least the four he had available to him. "So maybe Dibbs and his cat had been in the Notch trailer. And Dibbs killed Notch."

Morgan, who was also known for his tendency to jump to conclusions, slapped his hand on his desk. "You see, Grave, what did I tell you. Dibbs is our man."

Grave sighed. He had been through the captain's conclusion jumping many times before. "Maybe, but there's the little fact that Doctor Zorn had seen the cat in Notch's trailer before."

"Oh," said Morgan.

"And," said Blunt, "the cat had been scratching at Notch's door just before he disappeared on me."

June cleared her throat. "Sir, if I may?"

They all stopped and looked at her, or at least where they thought she was.

"The simcat would have been sold by Ramrod Robotics. All we need do is check the sales records to determine who owns it."

They all gawped at her, Morgan the first to accept the obvious. "All right, can you help us with that?"

"Of course."

"So," said Grave, "Whoever, or whomever, the cat belongs to is one thing. But what really are its capabilities and why are we having such a hard time finding it?"

"Ah," said June, brightening. "When we make a cat, we make a *cat*, with all the things cats are known for: stealth, wariness, and a fierce independence."

"But surely the simdrones could detect it."

June brightened even further. "That's the beauty of it. Why would we make a cat that could be easily found? The people who buy our simcats want them to be as real as possible. What fun would it be if they could find their cat whenever they wanted to? I mean, that just kills the mystery and mystique that comes with owning a cat."

"So why can't the simdrones find it?" said Morgan. "I thought they had state-of-the-art sensors."

"They do, they do," said June, "but not when it comes to cats. With cats, I'm afraid the cats win out. We installed a cloaking device that makes them invisible to all known sensors, other than a direct visual sighting. Really, captain, if we had wanted the simcats to be found so easily, we would have made simdogs instead."

Morgan threw up his hands. "Then what do you suggest? Do we just go to the trailer park and yell *kitty-kitty?*"

June seemed to be capable of unlimited brightening. "No, no, there's a failsafe of sorts. We didn't want the simcats to just go wandering off, so we installed a special chip that links them, binds them, to their owners. They're programmed to stay within a hundred yards of their owners at all times, and to check in with them at random intervals throughout the day."

"Wait," said Grave. "So what you're telling me is that the cat isn't at the trailer park anymore."

"Exactly, it's following the owner.

"Dibbs," said Morgan.

"Or Notch," said Blunt.

"So," said Grave, "it's either at the morgue or it's—

"*Anywhere,*" said June, perhaps too brightly.

Grave sighed. "Well, that's just great."

"Shall we head on over to the morgue, sir?" said Blunt.

"No, not yet. I need to finish up this interview with Doctor Zorn. Which reminds me, there's more than a cat missing. Notch's cellphone was nowhere to be found at the scene."

Morgan raised his eyebrows. "You don't say?"

"I can handle that," said Blunt. "Not the phone, but I can certainly get the records of his calls. That might give us something."

"Great, do that," said Grave.

"And I'll check out the ownership records of the cat," said June, somewhat less brightly.

Grave was about to thank her, but at that moment Doctor Zorn began pounding on the interrogation room door, demanding to be released.

Grave chuckled. "Our guest is heard from."

Grave went back into the interrogation room, escorted Doctor Zorn back to his chair, and sat down opposite him. "This will only take a few minutes, so settle down."

"This is *unconscionable!*"

Grave held up a hand to silence him, and Zorn reluctantly complied, slumping back in his chair and crossing his arms over his chest. "Get on with it."

"Good," said Grave. "Let's talk about the cat."

"Notch's cat?"

"Yes."

"What of it?"

"Did you see it when you arrived at the scene?"

Zorn looked at the ceiling. "No, but he *has* a cat and that's why I flushed the pills."

"And you're sure it's Notch's cat and not someone else's?"

Zorn threw up his hands. "How should I know? But the cat was always there on my previous visits. I just assumed..."

"That it was Notch's, yes. And did you know it wasn't a real cat?"

Zorn's eyes widened. "Why, no, I didn't." He laughed nervously. "I guess my scooping up the pills was all for naught."

Grave nodded. "Let's move on, then. When you arrived, did you see Notch's cellphone?"

Zorn looked puzzled. "No, I mean, I don't know. I presume it was there. He *had* called me."

"Okay, were you in frequent phone contact with Notch since his diagnosis?"

"Not really. He had regular office visits. There were phone reminders, of course, about upcoming appointments. And maybe a couple of calls when he thought he was having an attack."

"But you never initiated calls with him."

"No, just appointment reminders, and those would have come from my receptionist."

"So no routine contact?"

"No."

"All right, about poor Mr. Potz, where were you on the night of the murder?"

"Tuesday, you mean?"

"No, Wednesday."

Zorn shrugged. "I don't know, at home, I guess."

"And can anyone corroborate that?"

Zorn looked alarmed. "Now, see here, you can't *think*."

Grave smiled at him. "Just routine, I assure you."

Outrage had returned to Zorn's face. "I can't *believe* you'd think I had *anything* to do with the death of one of my patients."

Grave leaned across the table. "There is one thing that gives me concern, doctor."

Zorn met Grave's lean with a scornful lean of his own. "And what might *that* be, detective?"

"Your diagnosis."

Zorn sat back. "What about it?"

"You got it wrong."

Zorn was outraged. "So, now you're a *doctor?*"

"No, but I know a very *good* doctor, a medical examiner, in fact, who says that Potz didn't suffer from brain cancer at all."

Zorn chuckled. "Why, of course he didn't. He suffered from advanced pancreatic cancer."

Grave could feel the blood draining from his face.

34

Captain Morgan had been watching the interrogation, and didn't see a single thing they could hold Zorn on. In fact, to Morgan's way of thinking, the entire pursuit of Zorn seemed wrong-headed. The doctor was just doing his job, and that is exactly what Morgan communicated to Grave when he came out of the interrogation room. "We have to let him go. Seems like a dead-end to me."

"I'm not so sure—he has no alibi and there's the missing phone— but you're right, we have nothing solid to hold him."

Morgan signaled to one of the Morgan Freeman patrolmen, who immediately stopped what he was doing and marched over to the captain. "Yes, sir?"

"Take Doctor Zorn wherever he wants to go."

"Yes, sir." The simdroid started to move away, but Morgan caught him by his arm. "And record everything, including sound, on the trip. Then report back to me."

"Yes, sir. Shall I attempt to engage him in conversation?"

Morgan looked at Grave, who shrugged. "It couldn't hurt."

"Yes, sir." The simdroid moved to the interrogation room and escorted a still-angry Doctor Zorn from the room. Zorn gave them a grunt and a deep scowl and followed the simdroid out of the station.

"Well, he's a happy camper," said Morgan.

Grave chuckled. "He is." He looked around the room. "Where are Blunt and June?"

Morgan glanced around. "June went back to Ramrod Robotics to check the sales records. Blunt is here somewhere. Oh, there he is." Morgan pointed to a large cloud coming out of the men's room and heading straight for them.

"How did the interrogation go?" said Blunt.

"Not well," said Grave. "We let him go. Have you made any progress on the cellphone records?"

"I have them, but it may take a while to sort them out."

"What about voicemail?"

"None, I'm afraid."

"Well, I guess that's not too surprising. Notch seemed to be efficient and tidy, judging from his trailer."

"I guess," said Blunt.

"Okay, I know it's late, but why don't you start on what records you have."

Blunt looked crestfallen.

"What is it?" said Grave.

"Nothing, we sort of had plans for this evening."

Grave looked at his watch. It was already after six. "Then go, we can pick this up in the morning."

"No, I can stay. I mean, June is tracking down the simcat sale, so..."

"No, no, give her a call and have your evening."

"Yes, sir. Thank you, sir." Blunt moved quickly for the door.

"We should go, too," said Morgan. "I know I could certainly use some shuteye."

Grave smiled at him. "Yeah, me too, but first I need to see if I can catch Polk at the morgue. We need to retrieve the body of Mr. Potz and check out that pancreatic cancer diagnosis."

Morgan frowned. "It's not like Polk to miss something like that."

"I know, but he had no reason to look for pancreatic cancer. He was looking for brain cancer."

"Yeah, I know, but still."

"Yes, it is unusual for him. Anyway, let me give him a call."

Grave moved to his desk in the corner of the large squad room, slumped into his chair, and pulled out his cellphone.

Polk's phone rang and rang, Polk finally picking up, and immediately jumping down Grave's throat. "It's about *time*, Grave. I've been calling and calling."

"Sorry, what's up?"

"Are you sure you called Satin Passages about Notch's body?"

"Yes, of course. Charlize made the call."

"Well, when my men went to pick it up, guess what?"

"No, I'm too tired to guess. Just tell me."

"The body had already been cremated, and they said they never received a call."

Grave sat bolt upright. "No, that's not possible. Charlize made the call. I'm certain of it."

"Well, whatever the reason, we have no body to examine, so death by heart attack is going to be the only diagnosis that stands."

"Shit."

"Shit, indeed. Now, why were *you* calling?"

"Oh, it's about Potz. I just interviewed his physician, who says the diagnosis was not brain cancer at all. It was pancreatic cancer."

There was a long pause. "This whole day is going to *shit!* How could I have missed that?"

Grave didn't reply.

"So you want me to retrieve the body from Satin Passages, is that it?"

Grave could sense the frustration in Polk's voice. "Yes, we need to check it out."

"Well, welcome to the shit storm. Potz was also cremated this afternoon."

Grave wanted to say something more professional, but all that came to mind and mouth was, "Oh, shit."

35

Grave could see Charlize still at work on the Sprite as soon as the hovercab turned the corner and whirred softly down his street, depositing him safely in the driveway, albeit wobbly-legged and in a full state of quease from the journey.

Charlize was bent over the fender, her head under the hood, and it was clear from the ratcheting sound that she was tightening a bolt or a nut or some other gizmo that needed tightening.

"Hello," he said.

She finished her ratcheting with a grunt and emerged from under the hood with a smile, albeit a smile on a face marked by a war paint of grease. "It's wonderful, just wait."

"I hope not too long. Will it be ready by morning?"

"No, it's ready *now*. I think. Shall we take it for a spin?"

"Wow, that was fast."

She beamed. "Once I downloaded the instructions, it was easy. I just turned up the speed dial and had at it."

"Oh, I bet you did. Look, I'm pretty tired. Can we take our test drive in the morning?"

Charlize frowned. "No, you go on in. I'll just take her for a spin around the block—you know, to make sure everything is in order—and I'll be back before you know it."

"Okay, have fun." He started walking for the house, but turned back immediately when the gospel music came on at full volume.

Charlize pulled the little car out of the driveway and sped away, the sound of the choir diminishing only slightly when she turned the corner and disappeared.

Once inside, he went to the refrigerator, pulled out a half empty bottle of wine, and poured himself a glass. He sipped at it to make sure it hadn't turned, then walked into the living room and turned on the TV wall, which flashed to life with the images and sound of his father and Ida Notion being interviewed at the cemetery by Claire Fairly.

Grave slumped into his favorite chair, a tall-backed wing chair that had molded itself to his body over the years, and turned up the volume.

Claire Fairly stared alternately at the camera and his father as the interview progressed, smiling at the former and giving the latter her practiced "professional reporter" look of seriousness mixed with concern and curiosity.

"Mr. Grave," she said, "what's happening up there?"

The camera switched quickly to a view of the crime scene, where Grave could see himself standing with Captain Morgan, then switched back to his father's face. "A murder, Ms. Fairly, the dastardly deed of none other than Chester Clink."

Grave had forgotten how often his father used *dastardly.*

"And what makes you think that?" she continued.

Grave's father puffed himself up. "Why, I've been working on this case for years, and I know a Clink killing when I see one." He turned and looked directly into the camera. "It's precise and *gruesome.*"

Fairly moved her microphone from Grave's father to Ida Notion, who seemed smaller somehow on TV, even a full-wall TV like Grave's. "And may I ask who you are?"

Ida made her best attempt at a smile, but finally settled on a deflated frown. "I am Ida Notion, the renowned psychic, and I am assisting Mr. Grave on the apprehension of this, as he says, *dastardly* criminal."

"Ooh," said Fairly, "a psychic. And did your psychic impulses lead you here today?"

Grave's father stepped in. "No, we were headed here anyway."

Notion blustered. "But yes, yes, I did feel *something* as we approached."

Fairly was about to follow up, but Grave knew what would happen next—his arm entering the picture and separating his father and Ida from Fairly.

Fairly tried to object, but Grave already had the other two well away from her. "Well, then," she stammered, "this is Claire Fairly, Eyewitness News, coming to you from the Crab Cove Cinema Cemetery, site of a *gruesome* and *dastardly* crime, the supposed work of none other than the elusive serial killer, Chester Clink.

She stared into the camera for several seconds, a forced smile fading from her face, and then a commercial came on for droid insurance.

Grave finished his wine, set the glass aside, and turned off the TV, the sound of the commercial replaced by the sound of approaching gospel music, the paintings on the walls vibrating from the noise, until the music stopped and Charlize burst into the room.

She was beyond pixilated. "It's *wonderful*. Just wait until you experience the acceleration. And it will go three thousand miles on a single charge."

"That's great," Simon said weakly.

She broke from her reverie and focused on him. "Oh, Simon, you *really* are tired, aren't you?"

"You think? Yeah, I'm pooped."

Charlize frowned. "Let me get you out of those clothes and into bed."

She started unbuttoning his shirt, but he brushed her hands aside. "That's all right, I can handle it. Why don't you get out of those greasy overalls and shut down for the night."

She took a step back. "Very well, sir." She unzipped the overalls and stepped out of them, the full wonder of her body nearly toppling Grave from his chair.

"No, no, not here," he said, looking away and holding up the overalls in an attempt to cover her body.

She pushed the overalls aside. "Why won't you look at me, Simon?"

"Because you're perfect."

"Yes, I know, but if you think that, why not look?"

"No, no, it's just—it just doesn't seem *appropriate.*"

"Simon, Simon, Simon, you are so frustrating at times—and illogical. To look away from beauty, to think beauty is somehow inappropriate. It's ridiculous—and *illogical.*"

"No, it's just—"

"Been a long time since you last had intercourse. Yes, I understand that, and it's more the reason to reconsider my offer, with or without the additional programming."

Grave shook his head. "No, I don't want you to just *lay* there."

"Then I'll download the software. Which would you prefer, the six-position basic package or a more gymnastic one?"

Grave waved her off. "I don't want any package. I just want to go to sleep."

Charlize rolled her eyes. "You are so *exasperating*, Simon. You really need to get laid, and you know it."

"No."

"Yes, oh yes, you do."

"Do not"

"Do too."

This exchange went on for several more rounds, finally degenerating into "uh-huhs" and "nuh-uhs" before Grave's phone began ringing.

It was his father, and for once, he welcomed the call.

"Hello, dad, so nice of you to call." He waved at Charlize, who strode away in full pout and full nakedness. He couldn't help but watch her go. She was right.

"Simon, can you take me to the cemetery tomorrow. I'd like to sign the papers."

That was the last thing Grave wanted to do. "Can't Ms. Notion take you?"

"She could, yes, but I know you're better at this legal stuff than I am. I want you there."

He had a point, but Grave was still hoping for a different outcome. "Actually, I have to go to the funeral home, Satin Passages, first thing, so I couldn't pick you up until at least ten or so."

The prospect of delay had no effect on his father.

"No, pick me up first thing. I wanted to check out that funeral home, anyway."

"I thought you were using the other one, Wiggins?"

"No, it's part of the package price."

Grave began thinking about a different kind of package. *Gymnastic?*

"Okay, dad, I'll pick you up first thing."

Grave's father thanked him and clicked off, leaving Simon standing in the living room, looking down at the overalls that once held the perfect body that was Charlize.

He sighed. *Perhaps another glass of wine.*

36

Grave was happy to escape the house the next morning. Charlize's pout was still at full boil, made worse by the realization that he was leaving her behind. As she slammed doors and rattled pots in the kitchen, he quietly tugged on his clothes and slipped outside, forgoing even a cup of coffee.

The newly electrified Sprite was all she said it would be. It started up with an unfamiliar whir that was quickly replaced by a gospel choir singing "In That Great Gettin' Up Morning" at full volume. He backed the car out of the driveway, and sped away in a way the Sprite had never sped away before. He could tell by the clarity of the singing that the Sprite's old engine roar had been replaced by something approaching total silence. If he had had a way to turn off the music, he was sure the only noise would be the wind through his hair.

He looked around for the toggle switch that Charlize had promised not to install, and smiled when its absence was confirmed. However, there was now a new panel of very important looking buttons, each with a different colored light above it, some on full and some winking insanely. He started to push one, but then decided to leave well enough alone. He would have Charlize explain them to him when she was in a better mood.

Grave's father was waiting for him at the curb when he rolled to a stop.

"About time," he growled, climbing into the car. "Is this your idea of *first thing?"*

Grave ignored the comment and offered him a set of ear plugs. "It's even louder now that Charlize has replaced the old engine."

His father took the ear plugs and pressed them in. "Let's go."

The Satin Passages Funeral Home and Crematory, a low brick building surrounded by an immaculately maintained lawn featuring perfectly cube-shaped hedges on either side of its ornate copper doors, was the very image of clinical transport to the afterlife. Grave pulled into the circular driveway and parked at the entrance, where a man dressed in a shiny black suit awaited them.

They got out of the car and walked up the steps that separated them from the outstretched hand of the man in black.

"Good morning, gentlemen," he said, "I'm James Perkins, the owner and chief mortician at Satin Passages, your gateway to eternal rest."

Grave's father shook hands with Perkins, but Grave was less friendly, holding up his badge in front of the man's face. "Detective Simon Grave. And this is my father, Jacob Grave."

Perkins seemed startled by the badge, but then settled into his part as friendly host, clasping his hands in front of his chest and looking back and forth between Grave and his father. "How might I help you?"

"I'm dying," said his father. "Just want a look-see before I sign the papers over at the cemetery."

"Of course. And you, detective?"

"It can wait until we finish the tour."

Perkins fought back a frown. "As you wish. Come right this way."

Perkins opened the door and led them into a foyer that led off in all directions to what apparently were viewing rooms. Where the outside of the building had been spare and businesslike, the interior was pure unfettered opulence, from its velvet furniture, to its silk wallpaper, to its oriental carpets, to its brilliant chandeliers. It was the kind of showy excess you might expect to find in a bordello that was trying too hard. The place reeked of lavender and violets, with just a hint of embalming fluid.

His father was enthralled. "Wow, this is some place."

Perkins smiled. "Thank you. We do our best to make people feel comfortable. And if you're going to die, why not go out in style."

Grave tried to take it all in. "Yes, quite a place."

Perkins seemed very pleased with himself. "Thank you. Now, let's take a look inside the Skunkford Room, dedicated to our town's founder."

They followed Perkins into the room, which was dimly lit. At the back of the room were two figures, standing motionless. Perkins moved to a rheostat on the wall and brightened the room.

Perkins launched into his tour-guide spiel. "We offer a number of posing positions, from the traditional in-the-coffin viewing to something more lifelike. Here you see Mister James Thorlow, an auctioneer by trade, and his simdroid assistant, Bill. We've posed them as they requested, a scene portraying Mr. Thorlow at work, conducting an auction."

"That's creepy," said Grave's father.

Perkins took offense in defense of the choice. "Not to his *family*, and again, if you are uncomfortable with that, there's always the traditional pose."

"Yep, traditional's the way for me," said his father.

"Right, then. We can skip a few of the other rooms, then, and go straight to the Coffin Café."

Grave was incredulous. "The *what?*"

Perkins offered a businesslike chuckle. "Choosing a coffin can be a stressful experience. Seeing your final vessel, you see. So, we've made it into a coffee shop, where you can consider your options with a latte or cappuccino. And it's *real* coffee, gentlemen. Everyone *loves* it."

Perkins led them out of the Skunkford Room and down a long hall that opened into a room whose walls were lined with coffins of all sizes and levels of opulence, from plain wood to glistering gold. At the center of the room was a kiosk filled with the tools and equipment of the barista trade. A young woman dressed in a black blouse and slacks and wearing a red apron stood within, smiling efficiently at them. "What will you have, gentlemen?"

She looked like someone famous, but Grave couldn't put his finger on just who. He turned to Perkins. "Is she..."

"Yes," said Perkins, "she's a simdroid. We call her Angie, because obviously, she was made to look like that long-dead actress Angelina Jolie. In her younger days, of course."

"Remarkable," said Grave's father.

Angie cleared her throat. "So, gentlemen, what will it be?"

"Um, I'll just have coffee, black, two sugars," said his father.

"An Americano with an extra shot," said Grave.

"Excellent," said Angie. "I'll bring them to your table."

She turned and began preparing the coffees.

"Now," said Perkins. "Let me show you some floor samples of the possibilities." He turned to Grave's father. "Did you have a price range in mind?"

"Nothing too grand," said his father.

"Well, then, we'll stick to coffins under two thousand, then."

Grave laughed. "No, I think my father meant nothing too fancy."

It took a moment for Perkins to process the information, but then he offered an apologetic chuckle. "Ha, well of course."

He turned to Grave's father. "We offer a variety of less grand coffins, but remember, if you're signing a package deal with us and C4, we offer amazing discounts. You might be very surprised at how *grand* you can go."

Perkins led them down the line of coffins along the left wall and stopped in front of an ornate, gold-trimmed, ivory-colored casket. "Take this for example. It looks like it might be out of your price range, but in a package deal, it could be very affordable. And just look at her, a real beauty." He ran his hand across the smooth surface of the casket like it was a racehorse.

"Uh-huh," said Grave's father in a way that suggested he was not convinced.

"All right," said Perkins, "let's take a look at this one down here."

He took them three caskets down, to a mahogany casket trimmed in brass. "Or you could go with something like this. Very reasonable and very understated, yet powerful."

Grave's father seemed overwhelmed. "I don't know, maybe. Listen, do you have a brochure and price list I could look at?"

"Of course," said Perkins. "It's all a bit confusing, isn't it?"

"It is," said his father.

"Look, why don't you both take a seat at one of the tables while I go fetch our casket catalog. I'll only be a moment."

Grave and his father watched Perkins leave, then walked over to a nearby table and sat down. Angie was there in seconds with their coffees.

"What do you think, dad?"

"She's beautiful."

Grave watched her walk away. "No, I meant *this*, the caskets."

"Oh, it's overwhelming. I never thought it would be this hard."

"I know. Makes me want to not consider any of this before I die. Leave it for the living to deal with."

His father offered a *tch-tch-tch* rebuttal. "That's just like you, Simon. Putting off things. Letting others decide how you'll go out."

"Dad, I'll be dead. It won't matter."

His father sighed and shook his head. Grave half expected him to say "kids" in some exasperated way, but he just stirred his coffee, silent except for the squeak of the spoon.

True to his word, Perkins was back in a flash with a full-color catalog of their caskets. "Here you go. You can take this along with you. It shows every casket we offer, from least expensive to most expensive, together with a price list that varies depending on the package you choose with us and C4."

"Good," said his father, taking the catalog and flipping through the pages.

"Now," said Perkins, turning to Grave, "how may I help you, detective?"

Grave tapped his father's hand. "Dad, why don't you go have another look at the caskets."

"Ah," said his father, "privacy, is it. Very well."

He stood up and went to the caskets on the opposite wall, leaving the two of them alone.

"It's about Mr. Notch."

Perkins looked puzzled. "Notch?"

"You picked up the body of a Mr. Jimmy Notch yesterday."

"Did we? Well, I'd have to check."

"The body was supposed to be held for pickup by the morgue. We called. Someone answered and said they understood the instructions."

"Yes, so the body's at the morgue, then."

"No, Mr. Perkins. For some reason, our instructions were not followed and you cremated Mr. Notch, destroying evidence that might have led us to his killer."

Perkins began wringing his hands. "Well, I assure you, if we *had* received those instructions, we would have certainly adhered to them. We are *very* efficient in that regard."

"And yet you didn't follow our instructions."

Perkins was defensive. "So you say."

"Who would have received that call here, Mr. Perkins?"

Perkins hemmed and hawed. "Well, let me see. It could have been me, but of course it wasn't. Or it could have been my secretary."

"Can we have a word with her?"

"Of course." He stood and motioned Grave toward the hallway.

As they walked, Grave had another thought. "So, let's say you didn't receive a call. Why would you cremate the body so quickly?"

Perkins shrugged. "Normally, we wouldn't. We'd have a chat with the man's family, make arrangements, and so forth."

"So?"

"So, he must have had a contract with us and C4, which specifies all the details. We would have had no reason to delay."

"To facilitate payment?"

"Yes, I guess you could put it that way. I prefer to call it efficiency."

Perkins led him into a small office, far less opulent than the rest of the funeral home, where a young woman sat behind a desk, keying in information from a stack of documents next to her.

"This is Cindy, my assistant," said Perkins.

Grave was startled at first. She looked just like Marilyn Monroe. "A simdroid?"

"Yes, and being a simdroid, she has no capacity to lie."

He turned to Cindy. "Cindy, this is Detective Grave. He'd like to ask you a question."

Cindy stopped typing and looked up at Grave. "Yes, what is it?" she said in Marilyn's most seductive woman-child voice.

Grave stammered out his question, and Cindy giggled. "Oh, that's easy. I thought it would be a hard question, you know, like why is life like a tuna fish sandwich, which I just don't understand, but I do love gospel music and the Reverend Bendigo Bottoms. His voice is so deep and dreamy, don't you think?

Perkins interceded. "Cindy, answer the man's question."

"Oh, oh yes. Sorry, I do run on. The answer is no, I did not receive any such call."

Grave couldn't help watching the amazingly seductive way her lips moved when she spoke. He immediately thought of Charlize and all that was possible—even gymnastics.

37

He saw the two men come out of the building, and froze where he stood behind the square privet hedge next to the door, which swung closed with a click, followed by the distinctive sound of a deadbolt being thrown from within. He'd have to find another way in.

He watched as the men got into a tiny car and sped away, the sudden sound of gospel music making him reflexively jump. As the music faded, he heard another sound coming from the other side of the building. A car door was squeaking open. He glanced back and forth, scanning the grounds for other people who might see him, but there were none.

The distance between the hedge where he hid and the next hedge on the other side of the door was well over twenty feet, but he decided to risk being seen and darted for it, coming to a stop as soon as he reached cover. Another sound came from the building, the sound of a garage door being raised or lowered. Perhaps he could get into the building that way.

He pressed himself up against the side of the building and moved cautiously along it, finally peering around the corner to see what was going on. Two men were loading large urns into the back of a long black hearse.

"Do you have the paperwork?" one said to the other.

The other man looked at the sky. "Shit, do I have to remember everything?"

"Not my circus, not my monkey," said the one.

"All right, dammit, I'll be right back."

"I'll go with you. Gotta take a leak."

The two men disappeared into the building, leaving the rear door to the hearse open. He moved cautiously forward and looked inside. Three urns and a coffin. And a smell, a distinctive smell, but faint.

He jumped into the hearse and hid behind the coffin, curling himself up, his long tail held tight to his body. He was back with his owner at last.

38

Grave and his father arrived at the Crab Cove Cinema Cemetery in two states of mind. He felt lucky to be alive after his father became curious about the new buttons in the car and decided to punch one, which kicked the car into a gear only dreamed about by automotive engineers, hurtling it through a busy intersection with only inches to spare between life and death by T-bone collision. Grave's father, on the other hand, felt unjustifiably put upon when Grave expressed his anger in a way unbecoming of a son, and quite disrespectful.

The incident should have taken them to the cemetery in good time, but the shock of it had forced Grave to pull over to recuperate and give his hands time to stop shaking. So they had arrived nearly twenty minutes late for their appointment with Mr. Winter, who seemed pleased to see them anyway.

"Welcome back," he said with a slight bow. "Your papers are ready."

"Good," said Grave's father. "Let's get to it."

Winter led them from the reception area into his office, where a series of documents were arrayed on a long conference table.

"Whoa," said Grave's father. "This looks worse than buying a house."

Winter offered a quick, officious smile, then got right down to business. "Mr. Grave senior, if you could sit here, we can begin."

Grave's father sat down in the designated chair, the documents before him, as if he were the last stop on an assembly line.

"You can sit anywhere," Winter said to Grave with a wave of his hand.

Grave took a seat opposite his father, so he could watch the process.

"Now," said Winter, "you'll be signing various documents, but not all of these. It will depend on the final package you select."

"I understand," said Grave's father, pulling out the Satin Passages brochure. "I think I'll be going with Package C."

"Wonderful," said Winter. He began to pick up various documents.

"Wait," said Grave, "what's Package C?"

Winter stopped sorting documents and frowned at Grave. "It's a middle-of-the-road package, neither too expensive nor too cheap."

"And what does it include?" asked Grave.

Winter sighed heavily and picked up a document, which he quickly scanned. "Okay, firstly, it includes all the amenities of a traditional burial. Secondly, it includes a basic upgrade to include a three-minute custom video featuring photos and video clips provided by Grave senior, with up to one minute of additional custom footage provided by PostTube. In addition—"

Grave interrupted him. "Wait, what's PostTube?"

Winter looked at him like he couldn't possibly *not* know about PostTube. "I thought I'd covered this already. Anyway, put simply, PostTube is a website devoted to honoring the dead, including video obituaries, life summaries, and related videos supplied by the about-to-be-dead, as well as custom videos created by PostTube for use here at C4. Its services are part of Package C, which includes a number of additional après death benefits."

Grave couldn't help chuckling. "Après death?"

"Après death, after death, whichever you prefer," said Winter.

"And those would be?"

Winter glanced at the sheet again. "Let's see. Okay, your father will get a skydrone message of up to 32 characters during the gravesite ceremony. Most people go for something like 'RIP Jacob

Grave.'"

"Sounds fine to me," said Grave's father. "Keep it simple. I like that."

Grave wasn't satisfied. "What else? The first time we were here you mentioned an advertising program."

"Precisely," said Winter, raising a finger into the air, "and Package C does just that. At the beginning and end of his own custom video, we'll place fifteen-second ads promoting various products."

"Various products?" said Grave.

"Nothing outrageous, I assure you," said Winter. "Things like life insurance and various health products."

"But not cigarettes or liquor, I presume," said Grave.

Winter sighed. "Package C includes advertising by *anyone*. If you want to restrict certain advertisers or categories of advertisers, you'll have to move up to Package B, which is fine with me. However, it comes with a price. An additional $10,000 to be precise."

"Oh, hell," said Grave's father. "Promote porn if you want. We'll stick to Package C."

"Very well," said Winter. "So the way advertising works is that the advertiser pays us, C4, a fee, and three percent of that fee goes into an account for Grave senior's beneficiaries."

Grave turned to his father. "Dad, that's creepy. I don't want to benefit from your death."

"No, it's my decision, Simon. Donate the money away if you wish."

Grave sighed. "Very well, I guess we're going with Package C."

"Excellent," said Winter. "Let me just grab the appropriate documents, and we'll proceed."

He began collating documents, then suddenly stopped. "Oh, we forgot about the casket. Did you make a selection?"

"Actually," said Grave's father, "Seeing the caskets creeped me out, so I've decided to go with cremation. The thought of lying in a box, moldering away for all eternity just doesn't appeal to me. Okay, Simon, don't give me that look. It's *my* decision, so don't you say a word."

"But if you're going with cremation," said Simon, "why do you need to be buried?"

Grave's father pounded the table. "Because I don't want to be tossed to the wind or spend eternity on your mantle."

Simon slumped back in his chair. "As you wish."

"Very well," said Winter. "I'll just need this one more document and bingo-bango, we'll be ready for signing."

"Great," said Grave's father.

"Oh," said Winter, "and you're in luck. We're currently interring a number of urns today. Several ceremonies, in fact, are currently underway. Once you've signed the papers, you can see what your ceremony will look like."

"Sounds good," said his father. "Let's get to it."

Grave watched in silence as his father signed document after document, and wondered how long the irascible old man would be around, whether he would be able to complete his years-long pursuit of Chester Clink, and whether he was even sick at all. He had to persuade him to get a second opinion, if that was even possible. His loyalty to Doctor Zorn was rock solid. *Why*, he couldn't guess. The doctor, to Grave, seemed anything but competent, and seemed to be at the center of things, even though everything pointed to Jimmy Dibbs, who had apparently made a run for it, further implicating him in the deaths of Potz and Notch.

Grave needed to get back to the station, talk to Blunt about the cellphone records, June about the ownership of the simcat, and Polk about the results of the Sparks autopsy. And then there was Pippa Wobbly, who seemed forthcoming, but still, her appearance at so many murders raised questions, even given that she was a reporter. Maybe she took the cellphone. Maybe she had unseen ties to the murder victims. Another chat with her might be worthwhile. Dig into her background. Get to know her better. *She really does have beautiful eyes*, he thought.

But first he'd have to suffer through a tour of the cemetery, and drive his father home.

39

Mr. Winter led them up the path to where it split, one way heading for the older section of the cemetery, the other to "where the action is," as Winter put it, the field of obelisks and video monitors dedicated to extolling the lives of the dead.

"Almost there," said Winter, who could see that Grave's father was huffing and puffing from the effort.

"Thank god," said Jacob Grave.

Grave was about to add a signal of his relief as well—he was far from in shape—but just as they were about to turn and walk up the newer path, he caught sight of Victoria, sitting on that same bench on the path to the older section.

He turned to his father. "Dad, you go along. I'll be right with you."

"What? Where are you going?"

"I just need to check something. Won't be a minute."

"Well, catch up, will you? You should see this, too."

"I'll be right there."

Grave watched them walk over the rise and disappear from view, then walked quickly up the other path to talk to Victoria.

"Hello again," he said, sitting down next to her.

She smiled brightly. "And you."

"I have to say I'm a bit upset with you, the way you disappeared on us the other day."

She looked down at her lap, not speaking.

"And your boss, Mr. Winter, says he doesn't know who you are, doesn't have a docent named Victoria."

"Oh, that," she said.

"What do you mean, *that?*"

"I'm not a docent, and I don't work here, at least not for pay."

"But you said—"

"No, you surmised."

Grave was nonplussed. "What? Wait, you said you worked here."

"Did not."

"And you don't?"

"No."

"Then why are you here, all dressed up in those old-fashioned clothes?"

She shrugged. "It's what I do."

"What, are you like a volunteer or something?"

"You might say that. I like to welcome people. I'm kind of a guide."

Grave wasn't really listening. "And come to think of it, why aren't you in school?"

She smiled sweetly at him. "I'm home-schooled."

Grave didn't seem to be getting anywhere. "But what do you actually *do* here? Just sit on the bench?"

"Mostly, but I also walk around, greet newcomers and such."

"And your mother is okay with you hanging around a cemetery?"

She looked bewildered. "Of course, and it's not like she leaves me by myself."

"So she's here today, in the cemetery?"

"She will be. Would you like to meet her?"

Grave nodded. "I would."

"Well, then, come back at dusk."

"All right, I'll do that, and remember, we still need to talk to you about Eddie Sparks."

"Who?"

"The gravedigger that was murdered."

"Oh, him. Yes, mother has talked to him as well, so we would be delighted to answer any questions you might have."

Grave stood. "Okay, I'll see you at dusk."

"Wonderful."

Grave walked back to where the path split and looked back at Victoria, who gave him a little wave. He turned up the other path, crested the hill, and saw his father and Mr. Winter walking back toward him, both smiling. Apparently, his father had seen enough, and was delighted with his choice.

But his delight switched to annoyance when he caught sight of Simon. "Where the hell were you?"

"Just checking out the older section."

"Well," said Winter, "you missed our signature urn ceremony."

His father was effusive. "It was *wonderful*, really. Respectful and not too showy. And the videos were *remarkable.*"

"Sorry I missed it." He looked back and forth between his father and Mr. Winter. "So, are we done here?"

His father chuckled. "Well, yeah, at least until I kick the bucket."

40

Mr. Winter watched them climb into the little red sports car and drive away, the sound of gospel music almost unbearable. He retreated to the safety of the visitor center, where a crowd of people was milling around the lobby, waiting for the next presentation on the ins, outs, and après-death benefits of the Crab Cove Cinema Cemetery.

He made his way through the crowd, saying brief hellos to some, but mostly avoiding contact, making his way to his office, where the Jacob Grave documents sat neatly stacked on the conference table, the check for the down payment sitting invitingly on top. He picked it up, smiled at the number, and set it back down on the top of the pile.

He moved it all to an out-bin marked "processing," walked over to his desk, and sat down. He glanced at the clock. Ten minutes till his next presentation. Time enough to make the call.

He pulled out his phone and clicked over to speed-dial, selecting the number he was using more and more each day. The man on the other end of the line picked up on the third ring.

"Hello," the man said. "Is it done?"

"Yes, Jimmy," said Winter. "He just signed the documents."

"Wonderful, I'll get things ready here."

"Good."

Winter ended the call and stood up, straightening his tie and tugging at his vest. Time to persuade a new batch of the soon-to-be-dead, or STBDs as he referred to them. Business was good.

41

The drive to his father's house was uneventful. His father seemed self-absorbed, in deep thought, and thankfully, disinterested in the new buttons Charlize had installed, their functions, save for one, a complete mystery to Grave.

Ida Notion was waiting on the front steps when they arrived, looking her psychic best in a long black skirt and matching gauze-thin shawl held close despite the warmth of the day. She was one of those people who seemed never to be warm.

Jacob Grave came alive when he saw her.

"Ida, you wouldn't have believed it. The tasteful pomp, the understated circumstance—a ceremony to die for, literally."

Ida frowned. "Jacob, a man should not beckon his own death."

"Oh, but it was *that good*, my dear."

Ida turned to Grave. "And what did you think?"

Grave shrugged. "I'm afraid I didn't see it."

"Your loss," said his father. "It was perfect, except maybe for the cat, which howled through the whole thing."

A bolt of lightning shot through Grave. "Cat?"

His father laughed. "Yes, as annoying as it was, it was also quite comical."

"What kind of cat."

"Oh, one of those, you know, coon cats."

"And whose ceremony was this?" said Grave, poking his finger at his father.

His father backed away from him. "Whoa now, boy, what's this all about?"

"The ceremony, dad. Whose was it?"

His father looked down at the ground, trying to remember. "Oh, a Jimmy something."

"Notch?"

"No, maybe, I don't know. Why is this so important?"

Grave was already walking away from him. He pulled out his cellphone and called Captain Morgan.

"Captain, Grave. I think I know where we can find our simcat."

"Oh, and where's that?"

"At that cinema cemetery, next to one of the graves."

"There are a lot of graves. Which one?"

"At Notch's grave. Mr. Winter should be able to show you which one."

"He's already buried?"

"Yes, apparently."

Okay, I'll send a team. When are you coming to the station?"

"Soon. I have to make a stop at home, but I should be back within the hour."

"Good, Polk and Blunt and his wife should be here by then. Perhaps we can piece the whole thing together."

"We need that cat, sir."

"Don't worry, we're on it. Just get here."

Morgan clicked off without waiting for an answer. Grave pocketed his phone, and walked back to his father and Ida.

"Dad, I have to go."

"The cat thing?"

"Yes, it's not a real cat. It's a simcat, and we think it has video that could break this case wide open."

His father slapped him on the shoulder. "Wonderful. Now, you go on your way. Ida and I are off in search of that Clink mailbox."

Grave frowned. "Well, good luck with that."

Ida bristled. "It is not about luck."

"Yeah, I know, you have a *feeling.*"

"Don't criticize what you don't understand."

"Fine, but what is this feeling you have?"

Ida wrapped her shawl around herself even tighter. "It is not just the *mailbox*, Simon. I am getting mixed images, as if two murders are underway. I see crabs, everywhere crabs, and a name, Jimmy or James, a J name for sure."

"Maybe you see Jimmie crabs, you know, male crabs."

"Do not mock me, Simon. It's a man Jimmy."

"Okay, do you also see a Jimmy Notch, perhaps?"

She squinted, looking past him to some unknown spot in the universe. "No, I cannot make out the surname. It is lost in mist."

Grave scoffed. "Mist, huh? Well, in case you haven't noticed, half the men and boys in this town are named after the Jimmie crab. It's a tradition among watermen."

She moved from that distant spot in the universe to a place closer, where words came cold. "I know that, Simon."

"And why are you sensing a male name? Doesn't Clink prefer young women?"

"He did, yes, but that man in the grave may have changed things."

His father intervened, tugging at Ida to move her to her car. "Come on, Ida, we don't have time for this." He turned to Grave. "Simon, go."

Simon went.

42

Grave drove home, his eyes alternately focused on the road ahead and the new buttons Charlize had installed, one of which he knew provided an incredible boost of power. He was tempted to try the other buttons, but he feared one of them might be for an ejection seat.

The gospel music suddenly stopped and the welcome voice of Revered Bendigo Bottoms came on with another featured commandment for the day, *Thou shalt not follow the idolater, or an idolater be.*

"Brother, sisters, friends, I know you grow weary of my recent rants against idolatry and the graven images featured at the Crab Cove Cinema Cemetery, which are an affront to God. I know you're thinking, *Why not talk of something more interesting, like lust, Reverend?* Well, the time for that will come. Oh, yes it will, but today—today— we must talk once more of idolatry. You see, this morning, I had the honor to conduct the graveside funeral services for another dear friend, a woman who passed away long before her rightful time, and what I saw there appalled me. It seems our traditional cemetery, the Crab Cove Garden Cemetery, has yielded to the forces of capitalism and self-idolatry. Everywhere I looked, tasteful tombstones were being replaced by video obelisks featuring yet more graven images. Even my dear departed friend had yielded to pride and idolatry of self over God. No tombstone for her, no, but an obelisk taller than she was in life, with a video screen more suited for a sports bar. And the images—the images!—were an offense to God. Now, I know what you are thinking. You're thinking, *Reverend, we only have two cemeteries. What choice do I have?* Well, starting today, you have a third choice, the Crab Cove Holy Name Cemetery, a cemetery where the departed may rest humbly in the arms of the Lord, for a reasonable price. There will be no obelisks. There will be no video screens. There will be no graven images. Stay tuned now. I'll have a special offer on our burial services, coming right up after the next three songs."

The gospel music started up once more and then died almost immediately as Grave pulled into his driveway and turned off the ignition. Charlize was standing on the front porch, looking pensive. Grave sighed. He'd have to apologize to her.

He got out of the car and walked up the steps to the porch, trying to think of what to say, but Charlize beat him to it.

"Don't say a word, Simon. You were right, and I was wrong, and I won't trouble you any more about how to live your life."

"No," Simon said, "You're probably right. I just have to think it through and make a decision."

She smiled at him, came forward, and gave him a brief hug. "All right, then, how did you like the car?"

Simon was happy to change the subject. "It's wonderful, but you really need to tell me about those new buttons. My father pressed one and we rocketed away through a busy intersection. Lucky to be alive."

Charlize laughed. "No, you weren't lucky. That button activates a booster and a radar that allows the car to automatically accelerate without fear of hitting *anything.*"

"So we were safe all along?"

"Absolutely. Come on, let me show you the other buttons."

Charlize skipped down the steps, Grave in pursuit, and slipped into the passenger seat of the Sprite. Grave went around to the other side and climbed in.

She pointed at a button. "Now, this one on the end, the blue one, this is the one your dad pushed, so remember that."

"Right."

"Now, the two red ones next to each other are red for a very good reason. They activate ejection seats for you and your passenger. And just to be safe, I added protective caps over them, so you have to lift the caps purposively to have access to the ejection buttons."

"Okay."

"So that leaves the green one and the white one. The white one is easy, it activates a cloaking device."

"Invisibility?"

"No, more like your Sergeant Blunt. There but not there."

"So, fuzzy?"

"Yes, or cloudlike, and in the case of this car and its full-volume gospel music, people will hear it but not see it, and feel they may be in the presence of a fast-moving holy ghost."

"Ha!"

"Now, the green one is going to come in handy when you're busy thinking or need both hands free. It takes complete control of the car. It's linked to your GPS, so you can just punch in a destination and the car will take you there all by itself."

"I don't know about that one."

"You are such a baby. So controlling."

Simon shrugged. "It just makes me uneasy."

Charlize giggled. "Yes, I know. Anyway, the green button also activates the radar, so again, no fear of colliding with anything, regardless of the speed you set."

"Well, that's comforting."

"And there's more. The green button can be activated on the fly, even if you haven't selected a destination. When that happens, the car will continue on a straight path without input from you."

"What about stop signs and traffic lights and dead ends?"

"It's got you covered, no problem."

"All right, I really wasn't expecting all of this, but good job."

Charlize beamed. "Thank you, Simon. I thought you'd like it."

Grave smiled back at her. "I do, I do."

Charlize opened her door. "Well, then, let's go inside. I can whip up some lunch for you."

"No, close the door, we need to go to the station to discuss the murders."

Charlize frowned. "But Captain Morgan..."

"Don't you worry about him. We could use your analytical skills on this one."

She smiled and closed the door. "And I've been doing some more research on the deaths, Simon. Perhaps that could help, too."

"Okay, let's go."

Charlize chuckled and began pushing buttons on the GPS.

"No," said Simon, alarmed. "I don't want to do that."

But Charlize had something else in mind. "Did I mention that you can push the green, blue, and white buttons simultaneously?"

"No, wait!"

It was too late. She pushed the buttons and the car, now nearly invisible, backed out of the driveway and accelerated away, the g-forces pressing Simon backward in his seat.

He closed his eyes and hoped for the best.

43

Jacob Grave sat in the passenger seat of Ida Notion's hovercar and tried his best to be a good passenger. Ida had the car in remote mode, the car programmed to go up and down the streets of Crab Cove in a pattern that would take them through neighborhood after neighborhood in search of the Pinky Bloom mailbox they hoped would lead them directly to Chester Clink, serial killer extraordinaire.

Ida's job was to scan the mailboxes on the left-hand side of the road, while Jacob scanned the boxes on the right-hand side. At first, they had tried to carry on a conversation, but after a few minutes, they were down to brief reports on their failure to find the mailbox: *nothing here, not that one, nope.* And after an hour, Ida suddenly pulled the car over and stopped.

"This could take days, maybe weeks, Jacob."

He had to agree. "I know."

"Well, then, I say we do what I urged from the start: confront the artist herself, see if she can help us."

"Sounds good to me. We'll need to get her address."

"Not to worry. I've been there before, and we can get there in less than five minutes."

Jacob slapped his hands on his knees. "Let's do it, then."

Ida fumbled with the controls and punched in a GPS destination. The car hummed briefly, as if it was digesting the information, and then whirred away from the curb, accelerating as they went through intersection after intersection, Jacob—expecting the worst—sinking farther and farther down into his seat, his head well below the dashboard, his only view the sky and the occasional passing tree or traffic light.

But then, after only a few minutes, the car slowed and pulled into a parking space outside a pink and purple building that could only be the Pinky Bloom Gallery. If there had been any doubt at all, the mural of a giant purple crab on the front of the building would have set anyone straight on where they were.

Jacob tried his best to rise nonchalantly in his seat, but Ida was already chuckling. "Oh, Jacob, you're too much."

Jacob responded with a nuanced, somewhat defiant grunt, and got out of the car, Ida close behind him, and walked into the brightly lit showroom, which seemed to be alive with purple crabs. If you could put a logo on something, you would find it here: towels, shirts, sweaters, license plates, refrigerator magnets, ball caps, and yes, mailboxes. And there was more than just merchandise. The walls were filled with paintings and lithographs of purple crabs, each with a tiny price tag featuring a price with far too many zeroes, at least in Jacob's mind. And when he saw something he thought he might be able to afford, a little mobile of dangling purple crabs, the price drew his hand back from any temptation to touch it.

Jacob turned to Ida, who was admiring a sweater. "I don't think I could afford a refrigerator magnet in this place."

Ida dropped the sweater back onto the display table. "Yikes, I see what you mean. Come on, let's ask someone for Pinky."

They moved to the back of the shop, where a sales clerk was ringing up a sale, and waited patiently for her to finish.

"Yes, may I help you?" she said. She was giving them a look that Jacob had seen many times before, the kind of look a salesman gives you at a Tesla-Mercedes dealership when he thinks you are unworthy of his vehicle.

Jacob always had a response that put them in their place. He pulled out his old detective badge, which he should have turned in long ago, at his retirement, and flashed it in her face, which went from snooty to alarmed.

"Whoa, what's this?" she said, taking a step back behind the counter.

"Detective Grave," said Jacob, "and this is my associate, Ms. Notion."

"We're here to see Pinky Bloom."

The clerk grew even more alarmed. "Oh, my, Pinky? What is this all about?"

"Never you mind," said Jacob. "Is she here?"

The clerk nodded nervously. "Yes, in the back, but she can't be disturbed. She's arting."

"Arting?" said Ida.

"You know, *making* art. Um, purple crabs."

"Well, I'm afraid she'll have to interrupt her *arting*," said Jacob.

Without further word, the clerk turned and pushed through a curtained doorway behind her.

Jacob turned to Ida. "This should be fun."

Ida was about to concur when the sales clerk suddenly reappeared and held the curtain open for them. "This way," she said.

Jacob and Ida ducked past the curtain into a world of white canvas and purple paint. And standing in the center of it was a small woman in purple-splashed white overalls, a palette in one hand and a paintbrush in the other, hovering in front of a large canvas, from which a purple crab looked out on the world, claws open, looking angry, even for a crab.

"I call it *Angry Crab*," said Pinky Bloom.

"I can see it," said Jacob.

Pinky put down her paintbrush and palette, dried her hands on a nearby cloth, and extended her hand. "I'm Pinky Bloom."

Jacob took her hand, which felt surprisingly small and warm in his grip. In fact, everything about her seemed small, and thin. She couldn't have been more than five feet tall in heels, and had a head no bigger than a short-cropped, raven-haired cantaloupe, with beady, close-set brown eyes. Her nose was a mere slice of flesh, pinched tight at the nostrils over razor-thin lips that made her look muppet-like when she spoke.

"I'm Detective Grave, and this is Ms. Notion."

Pinky nodded at Ida. "So, what's this all about, detective?"

"Have you ever heard of Chester Clink?"

Pinky gave him a surprised look. "Of course, the serial killer, but what does that have to do with me?"

"We have reason to believe that he bought one of your mailboxes."

"Oh, detective, I've sold hundreds of mailboxes. Frankly, my assistants can't keep up with the demand."

"No," said Ida. "This is a special mailbox, not like the others in your showroom."

"Special, in what way?"

Ida described the mailbox, Pinky instantly recognizing the one she was talking about."

"Of course, yes, that was my first one, a prototype."

"Can you tell us who bought it?"

"I'm not sure. We sold it at one of my exhibitions. To a man, I think."

"Chester Clink?"

"No," she said firmly, then reconsidered. "Um, I don't know."

Jacob couldn't believe his ears. "You don't know what Chester Clink looks like, the most hunted man in America?"

"No."

"He's all over TV and social media."

"Sorry, I really don't partake of either. My art, you see."

As strange as it seemed, she seemed to be telling the truth. Jacob pulled out his cellphone and pulled up a pic of Chester Clink. "Here he is."

Pinky looked at the pic, her eyes growing wide, even for small, tiny eyes. "Yes, he was there," she said, and then grew alarmed. "So that's Chester Clink?"

Jacob nodded.

"Oh, my god!" she said. "I was *that* close to a serial killer?"

"Don't be alarmed," said Jacob. "He is quite particular in his choice of victims." He regretted saying it the moment he said it.

"What, like I'm not worthy?"

"No, no," said Jacob, trying to recover. "He simply prefers blondes."

Pinky seemed satisfied. "Well, then, now what?"

"I don't suppose you have his address?"

"Oh, I see where you're going, but no, he took the mailbox along with him. I mean, normally we would deliver the piece to the buyer, as a courtesy, along with a certificate of authenticity, but he was quite insistent as I recall."

Jacob gave Ida his best nothing-more-to-do-here look, and she nodded back at him.

"Well, then, I won't trouble you further, Ms. Bloom."

She gave him a curious smile, as if she'd swallowed the proverbial canary.

"What?" said Jacob.

"Oh, nothing, detective. Just an idea that's come to me for a new painting."

"Oh?"

Pinky giggled. "A serial crab killer."

"Someone who kills crabs?"

"No, no, a serial *crab* crab-killer."

Jacob raised his eyebrows. "Well, then, we'll leave you to it."

She extended her hand again and Jacob shook it briefly. It felt even smaller and warmer.

They made their way out of the gallery and onto the sidewalk.

He turned to Ida. "What now?"

Ida held her hands palms up. "Back to the search, I guess."

Jacob groaned at the thought. "No, let's go back to the house. I'm pooped."

Ida sighed. "Oh, all right, but we'll have to get back to it tomorrow."

The thought made Jacob cringe.

44

Barry and June sat next to each other in the station's conference room, waiting for the others to arrive.

After a few minutes of silence, June spoke up. "Would you like to know what I found out?"

"Yes, but save it until the others are here."

She drummed her fingers on the long, polished table. "So, um, Barry, do you think you'll be able to put the crib together tonight?"

Barry wasn't looking forward to an evening of Bolt A and Nut B construction, but he also knew time was growing short. The baby could pop out any minute now. "Sure, absolutely, no problem."

"Good." She went back to drumming.

"Right, I read the instructions last night, so it should go together pretty quickly."

She stopped drumming. "Barry, have you given any more thought to names? It would be nice to settle this before we go rushing off to the hospital."

Barry wasn't eager for another round of Battle of the Names. They each had their own ideas about how the baby should be named—family traditions—but neither would give an inch to the other. "Must we?"

June sighed heavily. "I suppose we can wait until we actually see the wee one."

Barry took advantage of the lifeline. "Yes, let's do that. We wouldn't want a Jonathan if he looked like a natural Alex, now would we?"

"No, we certainly wouldn't, and by the way, I hate both of those names."

Barry puffed out a sigh big enough to blow out the windows of the conference room. "Right, right."

June was about to offer alternatives, but the door swung open and Captain Morgan and the medical examiner, Jeremy Polk, walked in, the captain assuming his position at the head of the table and Polk sitting down next to him.

Morgan, clearly disgusted, slammed a copy of *The Claw and Mallet* onto the table. "Any word from Grave?"

"No, sir," said Blunt.

The captain glanced at his watch. "We'll give him a few minutes." He crossed his arms and slumped back in his seat.

"Would you like an update on the Sparks case while we wait?" said Polk.

"Good idea," said the captain. "Give me a sec."

He pushed back his chair with a squeak, went to the door, and shouted for Detective Snoot, who appeared in the doorway seconds later.

"Yes, sir?"

"Polk has an update on Sparks. Grab a seat."

"Or stand," said Polk. "This won't take too long. The man was definitely killed by Chester Clink. You just can't mimic the number, placement, and fury of those wounds."

"So not a copycat?" said Morgan.

"No way."

"Okay, now what about you, Snoot. Anything to add?"

She decided to sit down anyway, and took a seat next to June. "Well, Sparks was a psychic and therefore a threat, so Clink would have every reason to kill him, even though it did break the mold on his MO. But it's curious that Clink would just happen upon him digging a grave. Why was he there?"

"Perhaps checking it out for his own grave?" said June.

"Yeah, that's what I thought, too," said Snoot, "but the cemetery director, this Mr. Winter, said otherwise. Of course, I don't trust him as far as I can spit."

Captain Morgan and the others let that image arc across the room and splatter on the far wall.

"Holy *Christ*," said the captain, "can you *imagine* the videos and images that man would want to display?"

"Ugh," said Snoot, standing. "Anyway, if he was interested in the cemetery, he might also have been interested in a funeral home. Perhaps Satin Passages will know something."

"Sounds like a plan," said Morgan. "Okay, get to it."

"Wait," said Blunt. "I just had a thought, and I know it's ghoulish, but maybe Clink was there to view the videos of the people he had killed."

Captain Morgan's eyes attempted to become saucers. "Yes, of course! They would be like *trophies* to him."

Snoot cocked her head. "As good a theory as any I've got."

Morgan, whose movements had often been described as sloth-like, suddenly became animated. "Look, look, Snoot, go to Satin Passages and see what you can find out, then let's stake out the cinema cemetery tonight and see if he shows up."

"Yes, sir. Will do."

Morgan turned to Blunt. "And once we're done here, Blunt, I'd like you to head out to the cemetery and talk to this Mr. Winter. Find out exactly where Clink's victims are buried, and then hook up with Snoot. No sense our wandering around aimlessly."

"Yes, sir." He glanced at June, who was just realizing that the crib would not be assembled tonight. She rolled her eyes in a way that suggested both frustration and grudged acceptance.

"All right, Snoot," said Morgan. "Get to it."

She nodded, then waved at the others and left the room.

Captain Morgan glanced at his watch again. "Where in hell is Grave?"

45

Grave had never felt more relieved by the voice of the Reverend Bendigo Bottoms booming out from the radio as the world sped by in a blur. His eyes were still clamped shut in utter terror, but the reverend's words, however strange, were like a balm.

"Greetings once again, brothers and sisters. It seems my days more and more are filled with funerals, and though I have no problem with people making good time to the arms of our Lord, the number of deaths is alarming. Still, that is not what I want to talk about. No, what I saw this day with my own eyes has sent a shock through me. Let me explain.

"I was at a gravesite service this morning, and the casket looked like it was big enough to hold a horse. When I inquired about its size, I was told that the deceased had insisted on taking his simdroids with him to the grave, including his manservant, Bruce, and a simdog named Willis.

"My first inclination was to laugh, but the more I thought about it, the more troubled I became. Have we become pharaohs, setting ourselves up as gods, interring our slaves with us at the end?

"And these simdroids! I was told by a mourner that the manservant was assembled to look like a famous rock star, an idol if you will, then made slave, now interred with someone who would be as a god. Idolatry upon idolatry.

"And these videos, these graven images, do they not do the same thing, set us up as gods to be worshipped? Friends, friends, we need to think long and hard about the future of simdroids. We make them look like idols, but deep down, aren't they just slaves?

"I'll have more to say about this in the coming weeks. For now, let my words sink in. Reflect upon them as the gospel choirs sing."

The reverend clicked off and the gospel music roared once more, but only for a few seconds. They had arrived at the station faster than Grave had thought possible and, most important, he was still alive.

"Whew," he said, reaching for the door.

"Wait," said Charlize.

He looked over at her. A single manufactured tear was rolling down her cheek.

"What is it?" he said, confused.

"Is that how you think of me, a slave?"

"What? No, no, not at all. I think of you as a friend, a colleague, and a companion."

She squinted at him. "But I do your every bidding like a slave."

He tried to calm her. "Charlize, honey."

"And without pay."

"Charlize, you do have money. Mine. Who do you think pays for your clothes?"

That seemed to calm her, but only briefly. She just wasn't buying it. "But even slaves need clothes, Simon. And just look at me. The reverend was right. You had me made to look like a famous actress."

"I didn't have you made. You were already made. They just had to program you to meet my needs."

"Like a slave, someone to do your bidding."

"Not always. Just look at this car. This transformation was your idea, not mine."

"So you don't think of me as your slave?"

"No, of course not. You're my *friend*. A simdroid, true, but a friend."

She wiped the tear off her cheek and attempted a smile, which quickly degraded to a frown. "Well then, *friend*, I would appreciate it if you would let me contribute more to this investigation. I know things, and I can analyze things faster and more thoroughly than you can, or *anyone* can."

"I have no problem with that."

She reached for the door. "Good, then show me. Let me have full voice in this meeting with the captain."

Good luck with that, he thought. "Charlize, you know how the captain feels about simdroids, and besides, he's my boss."

She gave him a cold stare. "Yes, but the question is how do you feel about your friend?"

Simon gulped helplessly, like a fish spilled on the floor.

46

Grave and Charlize got out of the car and walked up the steps to the station house, pausing briefly on the landing to make way for Detective Snoot, who glowered at them as she raced down the steps toward her patrol car.

"Watch out, Grave, he's on a tear," she yelled back at them.

"When has he *not* been, Snoot?" said Grave, more to himself than to Snoot, who was already climbing into her car.

Grave turned to Charlize. "Come on. Into the lion's den."

"Lion's den?"

"It's just an expression."

"What does it mean?"

Grave chuckled. "You'll find out. Come on."

They pushed through the door and made their way through an unusually busy squad room. Men and simdroids were scurrying about, some in body armor, all looking apprehensive and serious. *Something's up*, thought Grave.

He could see through the windows of the conference room that Captain Morgan was there with Polk and two clouds that could only be Sergeant Blunt and June.

"Here we go," he said. "Go straight in and sit down beside me."

"All right," said Charlize. "Is this the den?"

"We'll see."

Grave opened the door and sat down before Captain Morgan

could say a word, Charlize sitting down beside him.

Morgan seemed to awaken as if from a dream when he saw her. "Get her out of here," he said without hesitation. "We have work to do."

"No," said Grave, as firmly as he could manage.

Morgan blustered. "What do you mean, *no?*"

"Sir," Grave began, but Charlize put her hand on his shoulder.

"Simon, if I may," she said. She gave Morgan an icy stare. "Captain Morgan, I have information pertinent to this case, information that no one else has, information that could ultimately lead to the apprehension and conviction of the perpetrator."

Morgan gave her an appraising look. "Do you?"

"I do."

Morgan smirked at her. "Well, sit back and wait your turn. We have information, too, information that could trump your information."

"I find that hard to believe," she said, "but very well, reveal your information."

Morgan nodded. "Thank you, *madam*. We shall indeed."

Charlize sat back and gave Simon's hand a little squeeze under the table. "Thank you," she whispered.

Morgan cleared his throat, and pointed at Polk. "What have you got?"

Polk seemed surprised that he had been selected to go first, but quickly recovered. "After some heavy lifting, I managed to get a sample of Notch's ashes. We're running toxicology tests on them now."

"Great," said Morgan.

"Maybe," said Polk, "but I wouldn't get my hopes up. Only certain poisons, heavy metals and such, would have survived cremation. Still, I thought it was worth a shot."

"Good," said Morgan. "Let us know as soon as you have something." He turned to Blunt. "What about you, Blunt?"

"Phone records, sir, but not much to report. Most of his calls were to an *establishment* in the Red Crab Zone, most notably, Simsex

Central."

Morgan grunted and leered at Charlize. "Can't say I blame him. I know if I knew I was about to die, well..." He let the sentence trail off to his fantasy world.

"*And,*" added Blunt, jumping in, "most of the incoming calls were coming from Satin Passages and the Crab Cove Cinema Cemetery, especially over the past week."

"Nothing unusual about that, either," said Morgan. "Final arrangements and so forth."

"Nothing from Doctor Zorn?" said Grave.

"Just the one call from Notch to Zorn."

Grave frowned. "I don't get it. If there's nothing to hide, why steal his phone?"

"Well," said Blunt, "there is one more thing I found, which may or may not be important."

"All right, out with it," said Morgan.

"There was a call from Ms. Wobbly, the reporter."

"So?" said Morgan. "Probably just doing her job."

"No, sir. That's the curious thing. The call was made *before* Potts was killed."

Grave sat back, stunned. Maybe her appearance at the crime scenes was not coincidental. "So *she* could have taken the phone."

"Hell, more than that," said Morgan, "she could have killed Potts *and* Notch. I mean, she was *there.*"

"Right," said Grave, "right." *It was possible,* he thought, *but what was her motivation?*

"Well, then," said Morgan, giving a quick, dismissive sneer at Charlize. "Unless someone thinks otherwise, I say we go get her."

Charlize shook her head. "It seems an appropriate, logical course of action, captain. My information can wait."

"Good," said Morgan.

"Wait," said June. "What about the cat?"

"Yeah," said Grave. "Any luck at the cemetery?"

"No," said Morgan. "Nothing, at least not yet."

"Well, the cat could lock this down," said June. "The video should nail Ms. Wobbly if she's the killer."

"Right," said Grave.

"So, it was Notch's cat, then." said Morgan.

"No," said June, "but that probably isn't important. It's the video that matters."

"What do you mean, not his cat?" said Morgan.

"No, sir, it belonged to Jimmy Dibbs."

It took them all a few beats before this new information sank in, except for Captain Morgan, who remained puzzled.

"Oh, shit," said Grave. "Then why is the cat at the cemetery?"

"It's following Dibbs," said June.

"I don't get it," said Morgan. "Why on earth would he be at the cemetery?"

June put it as simply as she could manage. "Because he may be dead, too."

Morgan's eyebrows shot up. "You think?"

"Yes, it's completely plausible," said June. "The microchip tracker would have survived cremation."

"Tracker?" said Morgan.

"An option for all human-simcat relationships. It assures that the cat can find its owner. Most people opt for it, for peace of mind."

"So find his grave, find the cat?"

"Exactly," said June.

Charlize cleared her throat, not that she needed to clear it—it was just a programmed mannerism. "June, your conclusions are logical, but there are other possibilities."

"Oh?" said Morgan.

"Yes, sir, beginning with the possibility that Dibbs could be very much alive."

"But that brings us back to why he would be at the cemetery," said Blunt.

"Does it matter?" said Morgan. "Alive or dead, he's apparently at the cemetery, or at least he was this morning."

"Right," said Grave.

"And there's something else," said Charlize.

Morgan sneered at her. "That so-called information of yours?"

"No, sir. And it's just conjecture, mind, but is it possible the Potts and Notch murders are somehow connected to the Sparks killing?"

Grave shook his head. "Clink? That seems a bit far-fetched."

"But possible," said Morgan. "At any rate, let's get going on all this. Grave, take Blunt and find Wobbly."

"Okay," said Grave.

"Wait," said Blunt, "I thought I was supposed to check out the cemetery again."

"That can wait," said Morgan.

"What about Dibbs and the cat?" said Grave.

"We'll continue to look for the cat, and we already have a plan in place for the cemetery tonight.

"Plan?"

"Oh, right, you weren't here," said Morgan. "We think Clink has been coming to the cemetery to view the videos of his victims."

"Wow," said Grave.

"Indeed," said Morgan. "Now off with you."

"Wait," said June. The words came out with an urgency that startled everyone.

"June?" said Blunt.

"Oh, my god, Barry," she groaned. "It's coming, the baby is coming."

Sergeant Blunt went as white as a cloud can go.

47

Jacob Grave stared out the window of Ida's car and watched Crab Cove fly by. He was going to miss this little town, a place he had called home for more than seventy years. As much as he had come to accept his imminent death, he couldn't help but wonder what changes would come to this town in the coming years. And if he grieved for anything, it was for this unseen world to come. He wanted to know what would happen next, to see it, to be part of it, including Simon's life. And that was just not to be.

Ida's voice brought him back to the moment. "Here we are, safe and sound."

She pulled her hovercar to the curb in front of Jacob's house and eased it to the ground. "We can pick up the search in the morning if you like."

"Whatever," he said, his voice almost a whisper.

Ida sensed his mood. "Now, don't get discouraged, Jacob. We're going to find him, I'm sure of it."

"You sense it?"

"Yes, I do. The images are coming more frequently, more clearly now."

Jacob brightened. "Really? What do you see?"

"The mailbox, of course, but now I see other things. There's a white picket fence, and he's walking on a flagstone path."

"Near the mailbox, you mean?"

"No, I don't see the mailbox now. He's walking toward his house, not toward the mailbox."

"So he's already killed someone?"

Ida shook her head. No, he's just returning home, and he's carrying something. A small suitcase of some kind. Black."

"What else?"

"That's all, for the moment."

Jacob sighed. "All right, then, Ida, I'll see you in the morning."

"Very well," she said. "About eight?"

Jacob groaned. His old bones could not do eight. "Oh, no, let's make it more like ten."

Ida wasn't happy, but grudgingly accepted his plan. "As you wish, Jacob."

He got out of the car and watched Ida start it up and float away, the car dipping down in front as it accelerated away with a deep whir.

"I won't miss *that*," he said under his breath.

He started walking up the path to his house, but stopped when his cellphone rang.

"Yes?" he said. "Oh, sure, no problem. I'll be here all day."

He put the phone away, walked up the steps, and unlocked the door. The smell of decaying pizza and stale beer greeted him when he walked through the door and plopped himself down in his recliner. He had tried his best to clean up the place, to put things in proper order before his death, but the smell of beer and pizza seemed to stay, as if it had insinuated itself into the carpet, the drapes, and anything else that could host a smell. It made him simultaneously sad, hungry, and thirsty.

He could use a beer, maybe two. He reached for the armrest cooler and pulled out a beer, a Jitterbug Red, a small-batch red brewed by a local artisan brewery, Dancing Crab. He had been working his way through their line of beers, including Waltz White Ale, Electric Slide Stout, and now Jitterbug Red, which was far too bitter for his taste. Two more beers remained, Two-Step Porter and Twisted Pilsner, and he wondered whether he would live long enough to drink them.

His phone rang again, and he fumbled to pull it out of his pants pocket, failing utterly. After three rings, the phone went silent, followed twenty seconds later by a distinctive beep. He had a message.

He debated whether to check it, but instead dropped it into his cup holder and took another sip of Jitterbug Red. The bitterness seemed to fade after a few more swigs, enough so that he pulled another bottle out of the cooler and popped it open. He was feeling better now, even eager to continue the search for Chester Clink. *A black suitcase*, he thought.

The thought pulled him out of his chair, to the card table he used for a desk. He sat down and began flipping through the case files. Had there ever been a mention of a black suitcase?

He wasn't sure.

His phone rang again, the sound magnified strangely by its location in the cup holder.

Go away, he thought. *Just go away.*

48

The scene at the station had been frantic as everyone tried their best to help two clouds, one pregnant and moaning, out the door and into their car. Grave and Charlize watched the car pull away and then headed for the Sprite. They would find Pippa Wobbly while everyone else would be working the sting at the cemetery. With Blunt out of the picture, Captain Morgan had decided to fill in for him and talk to Mr. Winter about the locations of Clink's victims at the cemetery.

"Well, that was exciting," said Grave. "I hope they get to the hospital fast."

"Yes," said Charlize, "although statistics suggest she has fourteen hours of labor ahead of her."

"Speaking of statistics, what were you going to say back there in the conference room? What have you found?"

"Oh, that. It hardly seems relevant now."

"Tell me. You never know."

"Well, I had a thought that Doctor Zorn might be our killer, which seems to be not the case now."

"I had him on my list, too, but tell me, what did you find?"

"My thought was that if he was the killer, we'd find evidence in the death certificate records. I was hoping that we would see his signature on a preponderance of the certificates."

"And you didn't."

"Right. For every certificate signed by Zorn there were three or four signed by other doctors, even for certificates where the cause of death was cancer or heart failure. So nothing points to Zorn in that regard."

"I see," he said. He reached for the door of the Sprite. "Well, we won't rule him out just yet, but it's good to know what you've found."

"Thank you, Simon," she said, "and thank you for sticking up for me back there."

Grave smiled at her. "You'll have to forgive Captain Morgan. He's having a hard time adjusting to simdroids."

"But we offer so much."

"You do," said Grave, "you really do. Now, let's get on the trail of Pippa Wobbly."

"I suggest the newspaper first, Simon."

"Exactly my thought."

They climbed into the Sprite, and Charlize set the GPS drive to the headquarters of *The Claw and Mallet*. "Simon, close your eyes and listen to the music. We'll be there in three minutes and eleven seconds."

Grave didn't have time to object, the car whirring away at blinding speed, avoiding cars hurtling at them from all directions as the gospel choir sang on before abruptly stopping in front of *The Claw and Mallet*.

"I don't think I'm ever going to get used to this," said Grave.

Charlize chuckled. "You're such a baby."

Grave frowned at her.

"What? You know you are."

Grave sighed, then smiled. "I guess. Come on, let's talk to Ms. Wobbly."

The Crab and Mallet was a family owned newspaper that had been publishing its weekly paper since 1789, the editorship passing from father to son or father to daughter for generations. Not surprisingly, the newspaper continued to be published in its original building, a stone, three-story box of a building bookended by massive chimneys. The building had been expanded over the years to make way for new technology and printing methods, but every expansion was designed to meld seamlessly with the old building.

In fact, entering its doors was like going back in time. Save for the computers everywhere, the place was all eighteenth century, from its furniture, to its wallpaper, to its period paintings.

Grave and Charlize walked up to the reception desk, the receptionist already transforming from her bored-employee look to her competent-greeter look.

"Yes?" she said with a practiced smile. "How might I help you?"

Grave pulled out his badge, which had the desired wide-eyed effect.

"Oh," she said.

"Detective Grave. I'm here to see one of your reporters, Pippa Wobbly."

The receptionist looked puzzled. "Pippa Who?"

"Wobbly."

She shook her head. "There's no one here by that name."

Grave couldn't believe it. "She's thin, about so tall..."

The receptionist gave her head a definitive shake. "Nope, not here."

Grave turned to Charlize to say something, but she was already headed for the door. Grave thanked the receptionist and raced after her.

49

Captain Morgan felt relieved to be out of the station house, freed from all decisions big and small, and on his way to this new cemetery everyone was talking about. Although he was excited by the prospect of finally capturing Chester Clink, he was also more than a little curious about the cemetery. His retirement was approaching, and after that, who knew how many days he'd have left. He was already accumulating the persistent aches and pains of aging and wasn't sure if he could even make it to his scheduled retirement. Two years seemed like an eternity.

He pulled up his unmarked patrol car in the visitor parking lot and walked to the visitor center, amazed at the crowds of people on the paths that snaked through the cemetery, as if the place were a theme park. He pushed through the doors and, after a brief stop at the crowded reception desk, worked his way down the hall to Mr. Winter's office.

The door was open, so he knocked lightly on the doorframe to get the attention of the man in white sitting at a bank of video monitors.

"Ahem," he ahemmed.

The man in white turned and smiled. "Come in, captain."

Morgan was confused. "You know me?"

The man chuckled. "No, of course not. Reception said you were on your way, so..."

"Ah," said Morgan, flashing his badge. "Captain Morgan."

The man stood and offered his hand. "Winter. James Winter. I'm the director here."

"Of course," said Morgan, shaking Winter's hand.

"Please have a seat, captain." He glanced at his watch, then looked at a monitor showing the crowd outside the presentation theater. "I have a few minutes before my next presentation. How can I help you?"

Morgan got right to it. "We have reason to believe that Chester Clink has been coming to this cemetery to view the videos of past victims."

Winter looked stunned. "Really? Oh, my god." He looked quickly from monitor to monitor. "You mean he's out there now?"

"Maybe. I have people out there now, looking for him."

Winter looked even more alarmed. "Not in uniform, I hope."

Morgan smiled. "No, undercover."

"Whew," said Winter. "I can't have uniformed police all over the place. Bad for business."

"Of course, Mr. Winter, and we can't have them all over the place if we expect to catch Clink, which I assure you, we plan to do—with your help."

"*My* help?"

"Yes, we need some help identifying the exact location of his victim's graves."

"Ah," said Winter, spinning in his chair and plucking a brochure off the table behind him. He unfolded it and pushed it across the desk. "Here's our map. All the victim's graves are clustered in our crime sector, C-1 through C-237."

Morgan was taken aback. "You have a *crime* sector?"

"Yes, the cemetery is divided into several sectors, depending on the deceased's occupation or the source of their fame or interests. We have sectors for singers, dancers, hunters, accountants—even policemen and mimes."

"Like a theme park."

"Yes, if you will. It helps with the tours and theme nights and also gives our clients a sense of community, of belonging."

A community of the dead, thought Morgan, looking down at the map. "There's a lot of graves here. I need to know exactly which ones are Clink victims."

"Oh, of course," said Winter, "that's easy." He spun in his chair once more and retrieved a file folder, sliding it across the desk to Morgan.

"What's this?" said Morgan.

"The list you requested."

"You had it already prepared?"

Winter chuckled. "I'm efficient, not prescient, captain. No, a reporter requested the same list a few days ago."

"What? Who?"

"I don't recall, but her name's right there on the document."

Captain Morgan opened the folder and looked at the long list of victims and their locations. At the top of the document was a name: Pippa Wobbly.

Grave and Charlize sat on a bench outside *The Claw and Mallet* building, trying to decide what to do next. Banners along the street, promoting Crabapalooza, the final musical event of the summer season, flapped in the wind. He had promised to take Charlize, who was a fan of one of the bands, The Soft Shell Sisters, a group getting increasing attention for melding bluegrass with neodisco to create a new category of music: Twango.

"Well," said Grave, "this is a fine kettle of fish."

"What?"

"Sorry, an expression for an awkward state of affairs."

"I don't understand. If the fish are fine and in a kettle, how is that awkward?"

Grave started to explain, but realized he didn't know how. "Never mind that. What I was trying to say was if Ms. Wobbly isn't a reporter, *what* is she, and more important, *where* is she?"

"Ah, from what you've told me, her most probable location is a murder scene. However, since there has not been a new murder, that possibility at the moment is a dead end."

Grave laughed out loud.

Charlize seemed mystified. "What?"

"You said *dead end.*"

"So?"

Grave rolled his eyes. He knew he couldn't explain it to her. "It's not important. Listen, I think we have at least a couple of possibilities to try."

"Not dead ends."

"Right, live ends, if you will."

"You mean live beginnings, don't you?"

Grave sighed. He would have to stay away from word play with her. She just took things too literally. "Yes, that's exactly what I mean. Now, first off, she gave you her contact information back at Notch's trailer, right?"

"She did, but I ran the address as soon as I came out of the building here, and it's totally bogus."

"Crap! Well then, we know she was an attendee at the conference, so I think we double back there and talk to the people at the registration desk. If she's not staying at the conference center, perhaps she's staying at one of the conference hotels."

"That makes sense, but if she *is* the murderer, it would seem a mistake for her to be so easily found."

Grave had to agree. "If that's the case, we might have to check out all the hotels and motels in town."

"Of course, she could be staying in someone's house or even somewhere out of town."

"You may be right, but let's start with the easy stuff first."

"Very well."

Without another word, she got up, walked to the car, and began climbing into the driver's seat.

"Wait," said Grave. "I want to drive."

Charlize ignored him, closed the door, and started the car, the gospel choir booming out.

Grave scrambled into the passenger seat, belted himself in, and closed his eyes.

Three minutes later, a badly shaken Grave nearly fell out of the car. "I should have kept my eyes closed."

Charlize was beside him in moments, and grabbed his elbow to steady him. "You'll get used to it."

"Never."

"Oh, but you will. It's actually fun once you realize that nothing can happen to you. Like a rollercoaster."

Grave straightened himself and brushed Charlize's hand aside. "Whatever. Let's go."

They walked inside the conference center and made their way through the marble-floored lobby to the conference registration desk, which was busy even now on the last day of the conference. They waited their turn in line, finally reaching the front, where a simdroid who resembled a former president smiled up at them with his orange face. His name escaped Grave.

Without prompting, the presidroid launched into its standard greeting. "Welcome to the 17th Annual Crab Cove Conference on Crime, or C4 as it was known in the law enforcement community, the most bigly conference on crime the world has ever seen, believe me."

Grave blinked at "bigly" and Charlize gave him a quizzical look. "I'm sure that's true," said Grave.

"It is *totally* true, and since we're in our last day of events and workshops, I can offer you a 30 percent discount, and I mean that's *huge,* particularly for a conference of this stature, which is unparalleled in the history of the world, trust me."

Grave almost had the name of this president, but not quite. "No, I'm already registered."

"The young lady, then?" it said, openly ogling Charlize.

"No, no," said Grave. "I just need to ask you a question."

The presidroid looked wary. "A question?"

"Yes, we're looking for someone who has already registered at the conference, a Ms. Pippa Wobbly."

"I'm sorry, I'm afraid I'll have to invoke presidential privilege on that."

"What?"

"The information is classified."

Grave couldn't let that stand. He whipped out his badge.

"Ah," said the presidroid, "a policeman. Everyone knows I love policemen and all first responders, but I'm afraid I still can't reveal the information."

Grave placed his hands firmly on the counter. "Then I'd like to speak with your manager."

The presidroid seemed to shrivel. *"Him?"*

"Yes, the manager," said Grave with his best tone of insistence.

The presidroid sighed, pushed his way to his feet, and lumbered down the line of simdroid registration officials to his left. Moments later, he returned with another simdroid that Grave recognized immediately, one who had been built to resemble his father's favorite comedian.

He was not overly tall, with a rounded tummy bursting from his long, suede-collared black jacket. He wore a hastily tied bowtie over a white ruffled shirt. His head was big and round and featured a shiny red knob of a nose set in the middle of his face, which was puffy and soft, with a slight pinkish glow.

"What's the problem here?" he said, stretching out the "here" in a raspy drawl.

"They want to know if—" began the presidroid.

"Yes, yessss," said the manager, forcing the presidroid down in his seat. "Stay out of this will you? You give me the willies."

The manager turned back to Grave and Charlize. "Now, who are you, anyway?"

Grave flashed his badge again. "I'm Detective Grave and this is my assistant, Charlize."

The manager backed away from the badge, gave Grave a steely look, then turned with a smile to Charlize, tipping his top hat.

"Charlize is it? Why, I used to know a Charlize once. An aerialist, Charlize of the Trapeze they called her. She was a sight to see. I can still see her on her swing, yessss. Sad, really, she choked to death on a cumquat."

Grave interrupted him. "We're here in search of someone."

The manager paid him no mind, but focused his attention on Charlize. "I have a bottle in my room, my dear. Perhaps we could lose this stiff and adjourn there for a little tête-à-tête."

Charlize frowned at him. "No, perhaps you have misinterpreted our reason for being here."

"Maybe, maybeeee," he said, "but we can *misinterpret* in my room just as well as here, yessss."

Grave interrupted. "Look, we're here in search of a Ms. Pippa Wobbly. We have reason to believe that she is registered for this conference. If so, we want to know where we might find her."

The manager continued to focus on Charlize. "He talks a lot, doesn't heeee?"

"I'm afraid I must insist," said Grave, stepping in front of Charlize, blocking the manager's view of her.

The manager tried to peek around Grave, but finally gave up. "All right, all right, what was the name again?"

"Pippa Wobbly."

"Pippa Wobbly, Pippa Wobbly," he drawled. "I knew a Pippa once, back in Sheboygan. Buck-toothed she was, and walked with a limp. One leg shorter than the other, you see. Kept walking in circles."

"Ahem," said Grave, clearing his throat loudly. "We're not interested in *that* Pippa."

"No, of course not, of course not. That Pippa was Pippa LaFong, daughter of Carl LaFong of Sheboygan, a man afflicted with gout. Foot as large as a watermelon most days, yessss."

Grave started to insist once more, but Charlize was way ahead of him, reaching over the counter, grabbing the manager by his shirt, and lifting him into the air. "Pippa *Wobbly*," she said as firmly as she could. "Is. She. Registered. Here?"

The manager was bug-eyed. "Well, now," he groaned, "put me down and we'll seeee."

She put him down, the manager backing quickly away from her and turning to Grave. "She's certainly had her Wheaties today, hasn't sheeee?"

Grave repeated the question: "Is Pippa Wobbly here?"

The manager straightened his coat and tie, then nodded at the presidroid. "Donnie here can help you with that."

"Thank you," said Grave.

The manager turned to Charlize with a grin. "You are a strong one aren't you? I'm in room 375, third floor, to the right of the elevator, next to the ice machine. You can't miss it. Just knock."

Charlize just stared back at him.

"Very well," he said, "I'll be on my way, yessss."

Grave watched him walk away, then turned back to the presidroid. "Okay, *Donnie,* is she registered or not?"

"A moment," Donnie said, clacking away on a computer. "I'm sorry, no one by that name is in the system, and I mean no one."

"But she must be," said Grave. "She had a badge when I met her, an official badge."

"I'm sorry," Donnie said. "Fake badge."

"But—"

"Stop right there. If she is not in the system, and believe me, a lot of people say this is the best system they've ever seen, then she doesn't exist."

Charlize stepped closer to the counter. "Can you tell if she is *staying* at the conference center?"

He leered at her. "Yes, miss. If she's not part of this conference, she could still be staying here. Give me a moment."

He clacked away, shook his head, then clacked away some more, again shaking its head. "She's not staying here, and she's not staying at *any* of our fine affiliated hotels."

Charlize looked at Grave. Grave looked at Charlize. They turned on their heels and walked away.

"How about a *40* percent discount?" Donnie said behind them.

They walked faster.

51

Jacob Grave stood at the window, laughing at the simdroid approaching his front door. He had never seen one quite like her, but was pleased to know that someone remembered actress Betty White, one of his favorites from the distant past. Jacob had been young when she was old, but he always delighted in seeing her on TV then, and on the early morning Vintage Classics Channel now.

He went to the front door, opening it before she had a chance to knock.

"Betty White as I live and breathe," he said, offering his hand. "Welcome."

She blinked at the name, but then gave him an impish Betty White smile. "Everyone says that, but my name is Shirley."

"Well, welcome, anyway. What can I do for you?"

She cleared her throat, a programmed habit. "I will be your hospice nurse when the time comes. Doctor Zorn thought it would be a good idea if we became acquainted. He's given me all your medical records, of course, but I am more interested in how you're feeling and how I might ease any pain, physical or emotional."

"I see," said Jacob, stepping aside and motioning her into the house.

Shirley stepped in and began sniffing the air. "Oh, my, I see you have a fondness for beer and pizza." She sniffed again. "And not bathing."

Jacob threw up his hands. "Guilty as charged. Come on in and have a seat."

He scurried to the card table, grabbed a folding chair, and set it down next to his recliner. "Here, take the recliner."

"Oh, no," she said. "Your comfort comes first. Please sit."

He sat down in the recliner, popped open the cooler, and pulled out a bottle. "Would you like a beer?"

Shirley sat down in the folding chair and shook her head. "Oh, no. Although I can process that liquid, I really don't like the smell."

"Oh, well, then," he said, putting the bottle back into the cooler. "So, I assume you're the reason Doctor Zorn called earlier?"

"Yes, I suppose so, although he may have other things in mind when he arrives."

Jacob looked at his watch. It was already past five. "Did he say when that would be?"

"No, not exactly, but soon, I think."

"All right. So, how will all this work?"

She smiled at him. "You're a man who likes to get down to business, aren't you? Very well, let me give you my standard introductory remarks, but please, interrupt me at any time."

"Okay, shoot."

Shirley straightened in her chair, chin held high, and began. "Firstly, I am a simdroid, as you have probably surmised, one whose purpose is to care for you as your disease progresses and your need for pain relief increases. But I do more than dispense medications. Think of me as a dear friend, because that is what I hope to be for you. No subject is off limits. No feelings or emotions need be suppressed. I will carry you, support you, through the stages of grief, right up to acceptance. I will be there when you pass, to hold your hand, to wipe your brow, to receive any last words or instructions you might have."

She stopped abruptly, raising her brows as if to say, *There you have it, any questions?"*

"I see," said Jacob. "It sounds good, but what happens if my pain becomes unbearable?"

She pointed a finger in the air. "Good question. You will be in control at all times, Jacob. If you ever wish to invoke paragraph 16c of The Euthanasia Act, I will be here to carry out the necessary medical protocols."

"That being?"

"A series of three shots, but don't worry, it will be completely painless."

"Have you ever had to do this?"

She paused as if thinking. "Only in 2.375 percent of my cases."

"Really, I thought it would have been higher than that."

Shirley gave him a big smile. "I pride myself in that, Jacob. My hospice skills are second to none."

Jacob chuckled. "Well, I guess they *must* be. That in itself is comforting. But tell me, when does this hospice stuff begin? I mean, I'm feeling fine."

"Jacob, you can begin whenever you wish. Today, next week— *whenever.*"

"Good, because I have some unfinished business I need to attend to, a case I've been working for several years now."

She nodded. "The Clink case. Yes, I know. Doctor Zorn noted your stubbornness in that regard."

Jacob was about to challenge that characterization, but his cellphone began ringing. It was Ida again. "I should get this," he said, standing and moving to the window. "Reception is terrible here, so the closer to the window, the better. Won't be a moment."

He pulled the curtains aside. Doctor Zorn was walking up the path to the house. He'd have to make this quick.

"Yes, Ida, what is it?"

"Jacob, thank god you picked up! I have a feeling, a very *bad* feeling."

Jacob listened, his eyes going wide.

52

When Captain Morgan called, Grave and Charlize had just completed their visit to the twelfth of Crab Cove's twelve hotels and motels, the Sleepy Crab on Bay Avenue, without a trace of Pippa Wobbly.

Why would she be interested in the graves of Clink's victims? The new information was puzzling, and whenever Grave was puzzled he got hungry. And whenever he got hungry, his food of choice was chocolate donuts.

He knew the closest chocolate donut could be found at the Skunk 'n Donuts on Main, so he punched in the GPS information, pressed the appropriate buttons, and closed his eyes, the newly configured Sprite taking them there in less than a minute.

They nestled themselves in a booth at the back of the shop, Charlize sitting opposite him as he devoured the first three of a dozen chocolate donuts, and took a long sip of simcoffee.

"That's better," he said with a sigh.

Charlize rolled her eyes and pointed at the rim of chocolate around his lips. "Simon, you eat like a child."

He wiped his mouth with a napkin, picked up another donut, and then set it back down. "Why is she interested in those graves?"

Charlize threw up her hands. "Maybe we have this all wrong. Maybe she isn't the killer, but for whatever reason is trying to find Chester Clink."

"An investigator of some kind?"

"Yes. FBI perhaps, or a private investigator."

Grave frowned. "Could be, I guess, but she's been at every murder scene, and for me that's too many coincidences. And why would she hide the fact that she's an investigator?"

"I don't know."

Grave took a bite of donut. "Let's take this one step at a time. First, the killing of Potts outside the conference center. I saw her at the reception, but she would have had plenty of time to murder Potts and double back."

"To establish an alibi."

"Yes, to be seen."

"Okay," said Charlize, "she's a suspect for that one."

"Right, now let's move to the death of Mr. Notch. Again, she's there, and again, she claims to be a reporter."

"But Doctor Zorn is also there."

"Yes, it could be him, but if Notch called him, it makes sense for him to be there."

"True, but there's the matter of the missing cellphone."

"*She* could have taken the phone."

Grave stuffed the rest of the donut into his mouth and picked up another. "We really need to find that cat."

"I thought it was at the cemetery."

"It is," said Grave, stuffing another whole donut into his mouth, "but so far it has eluded us."

Charlize wasn't sure what he had just said. She grabbed the box of donuts and pulled it out of Grave's reach. "Simon, you're never going to get rid of that paunch of yours if you keep bingeing on donuts."

Grave looked down. "Paunch?"

She could see that he was upset. "Not a *big* paunch."

He put his hands on his stomach. "But a *paunch?*"

"The beginnings of one, at least."

He sighed. "Okay, you're right. Close the box."

Charlize complied. "We'll save them for later."

"Right, where were we?"

"Notch."

"No, we're finished with Notch for the moment."

"So Dibbs, then?"

"No, let's stick with victims for the moment. Sparks would be next. Why was she at that grave?"

"We're back where we started, Simon. We know she didn't kill him. Clink did."

"Yes, but how would she know to be there?"

"She was interested in graves. My guess is she stumbled upon it while she was looking for the other graves."

Grave shook his head. "Another coincidence?"

Charlize shrugged. "What about Dibbs, then?"

Grave eyed the closed box of donuts covetously, then threw up his hands. "I don't know. Yes, he didn't like Potts, and there's the matter of the chloroform Blunt found in his trailer."

"And the fact that he's fled."

"Yes, there's that."

"But if the cat's at the cemetery, then Dibbs is at the cemetery."

"Or he and the cat are now somewhere else."

Grave looked at the box of donuts again. He and his paunch wanted nothing more than to grab the box back and devour the remaining donuts. "I don't get it, this whole Dibbs thing. He had a motive for killing Potts, but he also knew that Potts was already a dead man. And why would he kill his friend Notch?"

"Still, he's on the run."

Grave sighed in frustration. "All right, let's get on with it. Morgan wants us at the cemetery."

"The Clink operation?"

"Yes."

"And it's okay for me to go, too?"

Grave knew Morgan wouldn't like it, but he was determined to get Charlize involved, maybe even a formal position on the force. "Yes, of course. We won't be part of the sting, but we can certainly have a look around and see if we can find Dibbs or that damned cat." More than anything, he wanted to talk to Victoria again.

Charlize brightened. "Yes, sir."

Grave wiped his mouth and tossed the napkin on his plate. "Let's go."

As he stood, his phone rang. He quickly pulled it out of his pocket. "Maybe this is Blunt."

It wasn't.

"My father." He started to put the phone back in his pocket.

"You should take the call, Simon."

"No, it's probably just some more nonsense about Ida Notion and her *feelings* about Clink's whereabouts."

"But given his condition."

"No, I'll talk to him later. We have work to do."

Grave turned and headed for the door. Charlize trailed behind him, pausing briefly to look back at the box of donuts she had left on the table. *Take that, paunch.*

53

Say what you will about Captain Morgan, he knew how to conduct a sting operation. If Grave hadn't known some of the officers involved, he would never have noticed them as they went about their business as visitors, mourners, and cemetery workers. Everything looked completely normal, which was the point.

Grave and Charlize strolled past the visitor center and headed up the path to where it forked, one path leading to the new sections, the other to the older section of the cemetery. Dusk was still hours away, so he was not surprised to see Victoria sitting alone on her bench.

"Charlize, let's split up. You go left, and I'll go right."

"Yes, sir," she said, and headed up the path.

He waited until she had disappeared over the crest of the hill, and then walked to the bench and sat down next to Victoria.

"You're early," she said. "Mother won't be here until dusk."

"I know. I had other business, so I came a little early."

"Mother was looking forward to meeting you."

"And I her, and there will be time for that."

"You'll be here that long?"

"You never know. We're looking for a man and his cat."

Victoria smiled. "I love cats."

"Have you seen a cat around?"

"Oh, there are lots of cats here."

"Well, this isn't your ordinary cat. It's a simcat."

Victoria gave him a puzzled look. "A what?"

Grave chuckled. "I know. I had the same reaction. Here, take a look at this photo."

He pulled a couple of photographs from his pocket and held one of them up for her to see. "It's supposed to look like this one. A Maine Coon Cat."

Her eyes went wide. "Yes, I've seen it!"

Grave held up the second photo. "Have you seen him?

She nodded with delight. "Yes, that's Mr. Dibbs. He's here, too."

"Where?"

"Oh, I don't know. Here and there. He was talking to Eddie Sparks the last time I saw him."

Grave was taken aback. "What? Sparks is dead."

Victoria giggled. "Well, of course he is. Like Mr. Dibbs, and soon your father."

"What? Dibbs? My father?"

"Yes, Eddie said his spirit would arrive today. He predicts things, you see. Quite fascinating, really."

Grave could feel the blood draining from his face as a cold chill shot down his spine, and finding no remedy there, raced back up again, leaving him bug-eyed and frozen in place.

"You're, you're a *ghost?*" he stammered.

"Well, of course, silly. I thought you knew."

Grave was about to say something—his brain didn't know what— but the air was suddenly filled with simdrones, shouts, and gunfire.

He turned to Victoria, but she had vanished. *Dad*, he thought, *Dad!*

He fumbled for his cellphone, pulled it out, and tried his best to make a call. Instead, the phone lifted from his hand and hovered maddeningly ten feet above his head.

"Crap!"

He raced for the Sprite.

54

The trip from the cemetery to his father's house had taken less than three minutes, but when he saw the flashing lights of the patrol cars parked outside, his heart sank. He was too late.

He leaped out of the Sprite and raced up the path, pushing patrolmen aside as he ran. "My father!" he shouted at them.

When he reached the porch, the front door suddenly burst open and out came Doctor Zorn and Shirley, both being restrained by officers, who hustled them down the steps and into patrol cars.

Jacob Grave came out behind them, looking shaken but happy. "Well, there you are, *finally.*"

Simon gave his father a big hug, "Are you all right?"

Jacob broke from Simon's embrace. "No thanks to you. Do you *ever* answer your phone? And wipe that grin off your face."

Simon kept smiling. "Sorry, dad, I'm just glad you're okay. What happened?"

Ida Notion came out the front door. "I had a *feeling*," she said smugly, then broke into a smile.

"She sure did," said Jacob, leaning over and planting a kiss on her lips. "Mwah."

Ida blushed. "I had this vision of a black suitcase. I thought it was Clink's, but then it grew clearer. It was a doctor's bag, and the path the doctor was walking up was this one, to Jacob's house."

"So, she called me," said Jacob, "which saved my butt."

"So Zorn was going to kill you?"

Jacob scoffed. "Oh, he *pretended* to be here for what he called a pre-hospice examination, but thanks to Ida's call, I knew otherwise."

"So you stopped him."

Jacob shook his head. "I wish, but no sooner had he come through the door then he shouted "procedure six," and that damned simdroid Shirley locked my arms behind me. I thought I was a goner."

"But that's when I arrived," said Ida.

"Boy, did she," said Jacob.

"I don't understand," said Simon. "*You* saved him?"

Ida crossed her arms. "Simon, I'm not just a psychic. I have a black belt in karate."

"You should have seen it, Simon. Wham, bam, boom. It was over in seconds."

"Wow," said Simon, looking back and forth between the two of them. "Wow."

"Indeed," said Jacob. "Now, let's be going. They'll be wanting our statements down at the station."

Jacob closed and locked the door to the house, and they made their way to their cars, Jacob heading off with Ida, and Simon slipping into the Sprite and its loud but joyful gospel music. *Halleluiah,* indeed.

55

When Charlize saw Grave come into the station, she rushed out of Captain Morgan's office and ran to him.

"Simon, what happened? Where were you? You missed the whole thing."

She was absolutely beaming, clearly delighted about something, but Grave wasn't sure she was just excited to see him.

Grave nodded in the direction of his father and Ida Notion, who were just entering the station, along with Doctor Zorn, Shirley, and the patrolmen escorting them. "I had to check on my father."

"Well, I'm glad you're here. You'll never guess what happened."

Grave glanced over her shoulder. Captain Morgan and Detective Snoot were sitting quietly in the captain's office, defeated looks on their faces.

"You didn't catch Clink," said Grave.

Charlize frowned. "No, we didn't. I raced after them, but they got away."

"They?"

"Yes, Clink and Ms. Wobbly."

Grave was taken aback. "Wait, she was with *him?*"

"Yes, they were running hand in hand."

"That's odd. Why would she go with Clink?"

Charlize glanced back at the captain's office. "Snoot remembered something from the case files and found a picture of her. She was heavier then, but there's no doubt she's Clink's baby sister."

Grave was stunned. "What the—"

Charlize smiled. "I know. We should have been following *her* all along."

"But why was she at all those murder scenes? Only the Sparks killing makes sense."

"Coincidence, perhaps, or maybe she thought following us would lead her to her brother."

Grave shrugged. "Perhaps. Anyway, let's go talk to the captain. I have to bring him up to speed on the other murders."

"Wait, but that's my exciting news, or at least part of it. I caught the cat!"

Grave was delighted. "That's great."

"And that's not all that's great," said Captain Morgan, who had snuck up on them. "This little lady saved my life."

Charlize smiled back at him. "It was nothing, sir. I couldn't just let him stab you to death."

"It was more than nothing, detective. I've never seen moves like that."

"*Detective?*" said Grave, looking back and forth at them.

Charlize couldn't help giggling. "Yes, I've joined the force!"

"She's *Detective* Charlize now, Grave," said Morgan. "Snoot's new partner."

"No, captain," said Charlize. "If I'm going to be a proper detective, I need a last name."

"How about Grave?" said Grave.

Charlize frowned. "No, the name is Holmes, Charlize Holmes."

Captain Morgan rolled his eyes. "Good one. Works for me."

He turned to Grave. "Now explain to me why your father, that damned psychic, that Betty White simdroid, and Doctor Zorn are here."

Grave looked across the room. His father and Ida were sitting on a bench along the far wall, Shirley slumped next to them, clearly made inactive. Doctor Zorn would be in the interrogation room now, waiting for him.

"I think we have our killer, sir."

The captain looked confused. "What, you mean Zorn?"

"Yes, he just tried to kill my father."

Morgan raised his eyebrows. "Whoa, then you best get on with the interrogation."

"Yes, sir."

Grave turned to Charlize. "Well, Detective Holmes, would you like to observe?"

She chuckled. "Oh, yes sir."

The interrogation went long into the night, Doctor Zorn insisting on his innocence until presented with the evidence obtained from the simcat's video files, which showed he visited the Notch trailer twice, once to kill him and a second time to act like he was just arriving to help his patient.

"All right," said Zorn. "Yes, I killed him."

"Why do that when he was going to die anyway?"

Zorn smirked. "He wasn't going to die. It was a ruse."

"A ruse for what?"

Zorn paused for some seconds, wringing his hands. "It was a money scheme. Create a false diagnosis, kill them quietly so no one would suspect, and then collect their money in fees for the funeral home and the cemetery."

"Satin Passages and Crab Cove Cinema Cemetery?"

"Yes, it was Winter's brainchild, a way to increase business. I got more doctor's visits from my patients—the victims—and a kickback from Winter. Everyone wins, you see?"

"Except the victims."

Zorn smirked at him. "Yes, of course. But then again, they were old to begin with, and going out this way, at least they had the chance to put things in order and create a remembrance video."

Grave shook his head. "And you call that a win?"

Zorn looked away.

Grave pressed on. "So it was the three of you?"

Zorn chuckled sardonically. "Oh, no, detective. I think you'll find it's a much larger number than that."

"Wait, what do you mean?"

Zorn smiled up at him. "I'm only *one* doctor, detective. I couldn't possibly feed them more than a few at a time, and they wanted numbers, big numbers."

"So there are other doctors involved."

Zorn nodded. "Yes, but I don't know how many or who they are. Winter was very secretive about that."

Grave remembered Charlize's—Detective Holmes'—data on death certificates. It would take time, but he was sure they would be able to identify each and every one.

"Let's get back to the murders. So you killed Potts and Notch. Were there others."

Zorn shook his head. "Just Notch. I didn't kill Mr. Potts."

Grave wasn't surprised about Zorn's denial about Potts. Grave had another person in mind, too: Jimmy Dibbs. He had motive, opportunity, and means, including a large bottle of chloroform in his trailer. "Aren't you forgetting one?"

Zorn looked confused. "No, of course not."

"Well, it seems our little cat has a different take on that. Its video clearly shows you and Dibbs outside the trailers. He saw you go into the Notch trailer, so you doubled back later that day and killed him."

"No."

"And, just like Notch, I'm sure we'll find that you sent him off to Satin Passages to be *processed* like all the others."

Zorn looked down at the table, defeated. "Damned cat."

Epilogue

A lot had happened in the three days following Doctor James Zorn's confession. James Winter and James Perkins had been picked up almost immediately, and within hours had identified seven additional doctors who were in on the scheme, all with the first name Jimmy or James.

Charlize thought the case should become known as *The Curious Incident of the Cat in the Daytime*, but not surprisingly and very predictably, the case became known instead as the *Ten Little Jimmies Murders*, and the enterprising Pinky Bloom had been quick to market with a whole line of paraphernalia and tee-shirts, including a best-selling tee featuring the words WELCOME TO CRAB COVE, HOME OF THE TEN LITTLE JIMMIES and adorned with ten purple jimmie crabs, some with blood dripping from their claws. *I SURVIVED THE JIMMIES* and *JIMMY DID IT* also sold well.

As for the elusive Chester Clink and his baby sister, Pippa Wobbly—if that even was her real name—they remained at large and very much the targets of multiple investigations.

Grave had taken time off the next day to pay a visit to the hospital, where Blunt and June were enjoying their new baby. The delivery had gone well except for the first few seconds of its aftermath, the doctor and nurses unsure that a baby had been born at all. Where Blunt and June could be described as clouds or fog or mist, the baby could only be described as completely invisible. Only the baby's cry changed the doctor's mind, and once located, she could be seen as a slight ripple in the air when she moved, a shimmering or distortion of the light.

The long debate over the baby's name came down to who the baby looked like. She certainly wasn't an Alice or a Frieda, and the traditional naming schemes favored by each family wouldn't do either. In the end, the only name that seemed to work was "Ripple," and Ripple, or more affectionately *Rippley* or *Rip*, she became.

From there, Grave had driven to his father's house, where affection was also in the air. He found his father and Ida sitting on the porch swing, holding hands and giving each other the telltale goo-goo eyes of love. Grave wasn't sure whether this new-found love was the result of love itself or a side-effect of his father's reprieve from death. Not that it mattered, at least to Grave. He was just happy to see his father alive and happy.

After several uncomfortable minutes, he excused himself, and with some trepidation, headed to the Crab Cove Cinema Cemetery for a talk with Victoria. She had been there as usual, sitting on her bench, and welcomed him with a big smile—and his now lifeless cellphone. She confirmed that Dibbs had killed Potts, a little bit of evidence that certainly couldn't be presented in court, so the case remained open, pending DNA results on the items Charlize removed from Dibbs' trailer.

They talked for over an hour about life and death and what comes after, which Grave thought to write about one day. Then she took him to see her grave and its simple headstone, its inscription nearly weathered away: *Victoria Skunkford, 1751-1761, Beloved Daughter.*

Before parting, Grave had promised to visit her again, particularly when he was working murder cases. For her part, she was thrilled to be deputized, and said she could probably help immediately with cold cases and the Clink Case with the help of her new friend, Eddie Sparks.

Grave walked her back to her bench, said goodbye, and walked back down the path toward the visitor's center, where he could see Polk and several CSI teams preparing to begin the long exhumation work ahead. Grave now had a better sense of what Polk had often told him at the morgue: the dead have much to teach us.

He drove home bathed in the many voices of a gospel choir, a fitting way to end the day. Charlize, aka Detective Holmes, was waiting for him on the front porch, dressed top to bottom like the one and only Sherlock. Grave laughed at the sight, telling her all she needed now was a Doctor Watson, whereupon she called out, "Watson, I need you."

A familiar simdroid came out the front door, specifically a Simdroid 3000, Series 2, a series of simdroids that looked like an actor from the previous century, Peter O'Toole. When it spoke in the deep mellow tones of actor Richard Burton, Grave knew at once that it could only be Smithers, the former butler at the Hawthorn mansion. Only his clothing had changed. Instead of his butlerly tuxedo, he was dressed in the wools and tweeds of a nineteenth century gentleman-doctor.

"Yes, Holmes, what is it?" he said. Then he saw Grave, and smiled. "Why, if it isn't Detective Grave. So happy to see you, sir, and so happy to be working with you again."

Grave smiled at Smithers-Watson and turned to Charlize. "Does Captain Morgan know about this?"

"No, not yet," she said.

Grave smiled at them both. Interesting times lay ahead.

Other books by Len Boswell:

Simon Grave Series:
A Grave Misunderstanding

Other Mysteries:
Flicker: A Paranormal Mystery
Skeleton: A Bare Bones Mystery

Memoirs:
Santa Takes a Tumble

Nonfiction:
The Leadership Secrets of Squirrels

About the
Author

Len Boswell is the author of five additional books, including *A Grave Misunderstanding, Flicker: A Paranormal Mystery, Skeleton: A Bare Bones Mystery, The Leadership Secrets of Squirrels,* and *Santa Takes a Tumble.* He lives in the mountains of West Virginia with his wife, Ruth, and their two dogs, Shadow and Cinder.

Thank you so much for reading one of our **Mystery-Thriller** novels.
If you enjoyed our book, please check out our recommended title for your
next great read!

A Grave Misunderstanding by Len Boswell

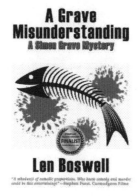

"The Bottom Line: A truly hilarious mystery in the tradition of Janet
Evanovich, Thomas Davidson and Rich Leder." —*BEST THRILLERS*

View other Black Rose Writing titles at www.blackrosewriting.com/books

and use promo code **PRINT** to receive a **20% discount** when purchasing

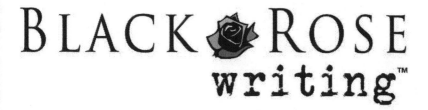

Made in the USA
Middletown, DE
20 October 2021

50671177R00139